# Mentor Me

## The Briarwood Chronicles

## Book One

*Logan Marie Schober*

This work is fiction, the characters, towns, and events are from the author's imagination and any similarity to real life people or places is coincidental.

Copyright © 2024 Logan Schober

All rights reserved.

No part of this book may be reproduced in any form or by electronic or mechanical means, including information storage and retrieval systems, without written permission from the author, except for the use of brief quotations in a book review.

Special Thanks to Cate Bleuel, Kaydali Clemente Avila, and Deyana Gorman for proofreading, offering suggestions, and being the author's personal hype squad.

To Jesse,

thank you for letting

me live my own love story.

*Mentor Me*

**The Briarwood Chronicles**

**Book One**

# Chapter 1

It has been exactly one month since I received my acceptance to Briarwood Academy. During that time, I managed to unenroll from Wilcocks High School, share a tearful goodbye with my best friend Sarah Mae, procure all my uniforms and supplies, engage in heated arguments with my mom about leaving the comfort of our small town, and come to the realization that if I want to become a world-renowned journalist, Briarwood is my best hope. To say I've outgrown the academics at Wilcocks is an understatement. Now, driven by that ambition, I find myself standing outside the imposing stone building that houses the admissions department of Briarwood Academy.

The admissions office at Wilcocks was less of an office and more of a table in the main office. At some point in time almost every student's grandparents or parents had passed through that office to attend the school. Don't get me wrong; Briarwood has legacies too, but the warmth and heart that emanates from Wilcocks doesn't exist here. The air is thick with expectation, every stone that holds the school together seemingly paid for by an alum who now has their offspring walking the halls. The students who graduate from these regal stone walls all go on to live lives of importance and wealth. Here I stand, a legacy yes, but unlike all the other students, my mom didn't graduate. She dropped out to have me. Now, the expectation in the air doesn't only surround me but runs through my lungs, pressuring me to live up to more than just that particular legacy.

As I reach for the ornately carved wooden door, it swings open, almost knocking me out with it. As I try to gain my bearings, out comes three girls dressed in the same blue plaid skirts and light blue dress shirts as me. Their blue blazers buttoned perfectly. Two of the girls are identical blondes with striking blue eyes, their hair set in soft waves around them. At first, I thought I was seeing double. It isn't everyday you run into twins. In the middle of them a shorter girl with sandy brown hair, pulled back into a tight ponytail and narrow face. She reminds me of a bunny rabbit.

"Excuse me," I mutter, still jarred by the suddenness of the door opening.

"Move it new girl!" The girl in the middle shouts. Apparently, she is less of a Thumper and more of a Bunnizilla.

"My bad" I half apologize as I step out of the girl's way and scurry into the building.

The admissions office is a simple room, only a wooden service desk with plexiglass is accessible in the lobby. It's similar to a bank. The stark white marble floors serve as a reminder that I am in one of the most prestigious schools in

Georgia. One could argue it's even one of the most prestigious schools in the country.

"Can I help you?" The light voice of a young woman behind the desk asks. She looks as if she has been crying, her auburn hair pulled back into a messy bun. Strangely enough she appears to be my age.

"Yes," I step forward. "I am Amelia Roberts. I'm here to pick up my class schedule. I received an email instructing me to report here first."

"Welcome Amelia. I have everything for you here. I'm Rose Childs. You'll find everything you need in this folder—your class schedule, locker number and combination, the name of your student advisor, your new student mentor, the student handbook, and..." She trails off as I look at her, feeling uneasy.

"Oh, am I going too fast?" she asks concerned.

"No, um, no," the words don't come easy, my throat constricts. I take the navy folder with the school crest on the front as she slides it under the plexiglass. I stare at the crest of the school. A gold seal with a B wrapped in thorns in the middle. I flash back to the nightmare I had last night of the thorns on the B wrapping around me. I inhale, filling my lungs and steadying my mind, letting the rising panic sink away.

Weakness is not something you want to show in a place like this. "I reviewed most of this information on the online portal. I'm just excited to have my schedule." Attempting a smile I continue, "The email said it wouldn't be finalized until my official start date."

"Very good, off to a great start. Don't worry I was nervous my first day too" she dashes my hopes that I was able to mask my nerves as she speaks. "I should warn you," she stops mid-sentence. "Well, I don't want to scare you, but the girl that was in here before, Lisa, Lisa Taylor. She's really upset that you took the last spot in the Journalism III class. It means she won't be able to have her minions with her. Bella won't take a class without Kate. It's a whole thing. So maybe be careful."

Confused, I ask "Who? How would me taking a class in my major cause an issue? The Journalism program is the reason I'm here. I was recruited." I don't like the idea of a possible enemy on my first day.

"I know. I processed your recruitment personally at the headmaster's request. It's a relief to have new students with us. You aren't the only one recruited this semester. Unfortunately, some of the returning students are upset about the influx of newcomers. They fear it will mess up the curve. Lisa openly advocated against recruitment at the last student council meeting. I have a feeling she won't treat any of the new students well, but you two having the same major will make her come for you. Especially with your recent success in getting published in several of the larger newspapers." As she rants the room starts to spin. My initial plan was to keep my head down and blend in.

"Do you know the background of all the students here, or just me?" I ask wearily.

"Oh, I know every student file backwards and forwards. It's my job. I have an excellent memory and organizational skills. It's why my work-study is here. I'm a scholarship student too." She pauses. "Sorry, I shouldn't have said that."

I hoped my scholarship status would be confidential, but it had occurred to me that once people found out who I was and who my mom was, it would get out eventually. "It's okay," I resign. "If there's nothing else, I should probably track down my locker before my first class. Thanks for your help."

I leave the office feeling no better than when I entered. I've already made a grave miscalculation. I thought at a school this size new students would be able to come in under the radar. Anytime someone enrolled at Wilcocks it was front page news, literally. The school paper would run an interest piece, something I fought against. I tried to explain to the other staff that there are people in the world who don't want to be the center of attention. The message was lost. The school would be in a buzz for days, everyone trying to get to know the fresh meat. Now I can only hope that some of the good karma I've collected advocating for those students' privacy helps me in escaping the same invasions.

Hope does me no good in attempting to navigate the halls. The school is enormous. I wonder if this is how Theseus felt in the Labyrinth as I attempt to move through the corridors before finding the lockers meant for juniors. My locker is D128, top row. I'm aware that there are people who would be elated over a top-row locker, but standing at only 5 '2", I have to reach on tiptoe to see the numbers on the lock. You'd think a school with this much money would have something other than archaic combination locks. Even Wilcocks High updated to Chromebooks, making lockers obsolete. I manage to open my locker and deposit supplies that I won't need in my first class. I might've overdone it with the office supplies. There is just something about shopping for sticky notes, pens, and the hunt for the perfect notebook that brings joy to my heart. Typing notes is fine, but I still prefer to handwrite them. When I shut my locker, I jump back in surprise.

Leaning against the locker set is 6' 2" of chiseled stone, and not the ones the building is constructed of. The buttons on his chest hold tight. I have to crane my neck up to see a jawline that could cut glass, and a pair of steely blue eyes staring down at me.

"Didn't mean to scare you, new girl. Just wanted to introduce myself to my neighbor." I study his face, but my eyes are fascinated by the perfect twirls in his curly brown hair. I continue staring, struggling to find words for the second time today. Unfazed that I have yet to utter anything beyond the yelp at first sight he continues. "I'm Benedict, but my friends call me Ben. Do you want to call me Ben?" The smirk on his face is the red flag I need to snap me out of my daze.

"Um, hi. I'm Amelia. Nice to meet you, Benedict." I respond by placing emphasis on his name. I know that purposely calling him by his full name might seem like a power move, but if I'm being honest, that smirk told me he isn't really interested in being a friend. I don't have time for a distraction right now, even if I want to find out if his curls feel as soft as they look.

"I'll take that as a no to calling me Ben. Fair enough, we just met after all. How about this, we can get to know each other when I walk you to your first class." Again, that smirk. I want to wipe it off. His voice drips with confidence even though he keeps a playful tone. Who does this guy think he is?

"I can actually get there on my own," I lie. I'm completely aware that if I were Theseus I'd succumb to demise by minotaur. "and I'm supposed to be meeting my student mentor." I open my folder to find the name and... well, crap. "Any chance there's another Benedict nearby or—"

"Benedict Blake at your service, Amelia Roberts, and no. I'm the only Benedict at this school." He continues to smile down at me. Demise by mentor a more accurate description. I'm already tired of having to crane my neck up to look him in the eye. Just as I'm ready to inform him I will be seeing my advisor about this mistake and ask for a female mentor, he suddenly takes my bag from the ground and slings it effortlessly over his shoulder. "Now, how about that walk?"

Internally, I groan. All plans of a hasty exit thwarted leaving me no choice but to follow him down the hallway toward what I hope is my first class.

# Chapter 2

I have to rush after Benedict to catch up; he has a long stride. I wonder… nope, don't go there Amelia. "Chasing after me already? I knew you would come around," he gloats.

"Actually, I'm just trying to catch the thief who took my bag," I counter, tugging my backpack out of his grasp, a bit out of breath. He jerks the bag, pulling my body into his firm chest. His free hand catches the small of my back and I emit a sound that is supposed to be an 'oof' but comes out throatier than intended. I quickly push away from him.

"Now, now, Miss Roberts, what kind of respectable young gentleman would I be if I let the new girl carry her bag on her first day?" His voice carries a false seriousness that reminds me of a character from a period romance novel. Barf. How am I supposed to make it through an entire semester with this guy as my mentor? I decide to play into his hand for a moment. Only for a moment.

"Well now, Mr. Blake, a respectable young lady cannot be seen with a gentleman on a promenade after only our first meeting, so I will just have to take my things and go." I smile sweetly, letting the sarcasm drip from my voice. Then I attempt to take my bag again, but he pulls back.

"Okay, okay, I get it. I'll stop, but I cannot in good conscience let you carry this bag. It weighs a ton. What do you have in here? The whole library?" His face is a mask of seriousness.

"Yes," I deadpan.

"Just yes?" he quizzes. I stare at him in response. As much as I would love to spend my time bantering with the future star of a romcom, I have to get to class, and so far, not much mentoring has happened. Even though I'm confident a guy who looks like this could mentor me on several things. Amelia Jane Roberts! Stop it right now. You do not have time for boys; you only have time for writing and, in the unlikely event you have a moment, more writing. Mr. Romcom takes my silence as an opportunity to continue his attempt at—I'm not actually sure what he is attempting, but his voice is annoyingly intriguing. "Okay, here is the deal. You are new, so of course I have to at least take a shot. But before you go to your first class, there are some things you should know."

"Deciding to fulfill your mentor duties now?" I raise an eyebrow.

"Like I have a choice." I almost ask, but he continues, "Classes here are set up similar to a university. You take 12 to 15 credits per semester depending on your ability level. The 12 is just there to appease the state requirements; everyone takes 15." He pulls a paper from his pocket and begins to read. The smirk returns. "You have all AP classes, Miss Overachiever, so keep in mind that your caseload is especially tough. Calc 1, Mrs. Rollins; American Literature, Mr. Laurance;, Journalism III;, Mr. Bannerman, Anatomy I;, Dr. Jones, and finally…" confusion lingers on his face. "Golf? You play golf?"

Embarrassment floods me. Of course I don't play golf! However, like most schools, physical education is required for graduation. I avoided P.E at all costs at Wilcocks. The thought of running in front of someone was enough for me to give up all my dreams of journalistic success and hide in my room forever. However, Briarwood requires me to complete the class my first semester, so I chose golf from the catalog. It seemed like a safe choice, walking, preferably in solitude, hitting a ball. How hard could it be? "Isn't that the purpose of the class? So I can learn?" I question.

Benedict shakes off his look of surprise. It's clear he wants to say something but is painfully refraining. "Sure, anyway, you don't go to every class each day. You have Calc and Lit Mondays and Wednesdays. Anatomy and Journalism Tuesdays and Thursdays. Golf on Fridays. You have weekends off to study and do whatever. Lunch break between classes. I'll meet you here between class changes to make sure you get everywhere today without an escape attempt."

"Escape attempt?" Is this guy for real?

"You'd be surprised how overwhelmed new students get with the course load. You aren't in Kansas anymore, Dorothy."

"Well, as long as I have my own personal straw man to help." I wisp out like a doe-eyed damsel. At this point, we've made it to the math department. I can tell from the large plaque on the wall dedicating the department to whom I assume is an old dead guy that gave the school an obscene amount of money.

"Just watch out for flying monkeys." he leans in a little and whispers "By flying monkeys, I mean bitchy third years, who are pissed you're messing up the curve." Shivers run down my spine as he leans back "Student records don't really stay private here. There's a good chance you have already made enemies just by being a part of the recruitment program. Also, sit in the back, resist the urge to be the good little girl in the front row. Mrs. Rollins spits when she talks." He holds a serious tone up until he says good little girl, and the teasing voice from earlier returns.

"What makes you think I'm a good little girl?" My mouth works faster than my filter and I regret the words as soon as they leave my mouth. Suddenly those intense eyes bare into my own blues as Benedict takes a step closer.

"I know my good girl is eager to please on her first day." I watch his Adam's apple bop up and down. I feel the air become thick with a different type of expectation and it is officially time to remove myself from his presence.

"I'm not your girl. I'm your mentee. Thanks for getting me to class." I turn heel and walk into the half-full classroom. Despite my racing heartbeat, I head calmly to the back of the room and take a seat. I want to purposely defy Benedict by sitting in the front, because darn him if he isn't right, I would have sat there. When I am settled, I glance up to the doorway where I left Benedict standing. His smirk returns, and he mouths "good girl." I am so screwed.

# Chapter 3

Have I mentioned that I'm at this school for Journalism? That point should be made crystal clear before I say, I hate Calculus, and the feeling is mutual. Mrs. Rollins does spit when she talks, and sitting in the back doesn't guarantee safety. The slim woman moves through the aisles as she lectures. Her brown hair pulled into a tight bun; she could pass as a ballerina the way she glides around the room. She is elegant and beautiful.

The only thing that separates her from a ballerina is the speed she talks. There's no grace in her voice or for her students as she writes on an electronic pad and notes appear on the smartboard in the front of the room. The first ten minutes gave me false hope that this class wouldn't be difficult. Simple introductions and the ceremonial passing out of the syllabus. However, as soon as the last student received their syllabus, it was straight into material.

The block scheduling keeps me here for a full two hours. That is two hours of taking non-stop notes, while trying to track Mrs. Rollins' movements in order to duck around any spit that comes flying out as she talks. It could be a sport. Maybe I can get out of taking golf and count this as my P.E credit. Probably not.

The sound of a bell has never been so sweet. One benefit of my entire focus being on the lesson is that I was able to evade any thoughts of my mentor. The small reprieve ends quickly as Benedict lingers by the door of the classroom. I attempt to slip out in a group of taller students, hoping that my small stature goes unnoticed, but have no such luck. Before I can get fully into the hall, the weight of my backpack is lifted from the shoulder I had it slung over. "Avoid the splash zone Dorothy?" His familiar playful tone makes it seem like we are lifelong friends, or another type of relationship I don't have time for.

"The whole classroom may as well be the stadium at SeaWorld setup on rotation the way she moves around." I hate admitting he was right, so I won't tell him it wasn't as bad in the back of the room. "I can break for lunch now, right?" I follow alongside him as we walk through the halls.

"Tapping out so soon? What happened to all the feistiness from earlier; I could loan you my notes from last year." Would accepting help this early be a sign of weakness? He is supposed to be mentoring me.

"Actually, that would be great." I take a chance.

His face emits a surprised look, but he quickly recovers. "Yeah? You can come over to my place, and I can give them to you." The implication makes it clear the gesture was not genuine.

"On second thought, no thanks." I roll my eyes and walk ahead. The cafeteria entrance is in line of sight. I walk a little faster. Darn his long legs, he matches my pace.

"Told you new girl, had to shoot my shot." His smile comes from the corner of his mouth now. It would be charming if I didn't have that pesky red flag blocking my vision. He stops just at the cafeteria door entrance. "You've made it safely. Your lunch number is in your welcome packet. Lunch is covered in tuition, so no need to load an account. I'll pick you up here before time to go to your next class. Lunch hour is the most relaxed time here. You can eat in the cafeteria, courtyard, or library. Students find themselves all over. Feel free to go anywhere; just be back here 15 minutes until class change. Your next class is a trek." He slips my backpack off and passes it to me.

"You're leaving me?" I don't mean to sound panicked. I'm glad to be rid of him, honestly, but he is the only person that I know. If you don't count Lisa. However, seeing how she and I have not been formally introduced and she's already upset about me being here, I can guess a lunch invitation won't be extended. I miss Sarah Mae.

"Awe. Are you going to miss me Dorothy?" he leans in, and that smirk makes my heart skip. It skips, okay. His eyes narrowed as he looks over my shoulder and half whispers, "No, just scared of the flying monkeys."

"I am not afra—" Before I can get the rest of the words out, I am literally pushed aside. After I recover, I get a nice view of brown flowy curls. The curls are attached to a curvy girl, with a skirt just long enough to cover her butt, and definitely not long enough to be in dress code. I can't see her face but Benedict looks dismal.

"Benny Boo" She coos. "Why didn't you text me to meet you for lunch?" She reaches up and twirls one of his perfect curls around her finger. I catch a glimpse of red nail polish. Ick. He visibly flinches from her. Not my flying monkey, not my circus. Figures Mr. Romcom has a hoard of girls. I bet she is an expired flavor of the week. Again, not my business but a good time to make an exit.

I slip away and enter the lunchroom. It looks like the Great Hall in Harry Potter. Just like it. Paintings cover the walls. They aren't of old white men, like you would expect in a place like this. Instead, Renaissance-style art, in beautiful gold frames. I could study them for hours and not get to each one. Wooden tables span the length of the room. Despite my abhorrence for crowds, this could easily become my favorite place to study. As I walk through the lunch line, I'm even more impressed with the food. Apparently, the culinary program helps prepare the meals. Wow. Once my tray is filled with roast beef, roasted carrots, and a potato mash (yes, the pretension even extends to the lunch menu), I find a seat away from the crowds near the end of a long table.

I shuffle through my bag and pull out my Kindle. Kindle rested on the table and fork in one hand, I become immersed as I eat. Oh my. This food is amazing. The writer in me wants to think of a better word, but I'm too encapsulated to care. There, encapsulated. That's a good word. It isn't until a hand jerks my tray away from me that I break the trance I've fallen under. Looking up I see Lisa and the twin girls from the office earlier standing over me. They appear to be attempting a version of the Charlie's Angels pose and failing. I would snicker if they didn't look so angry. Well, here we go.

Here's the thing about mean girls: the bigger the bark, the bigger the insecurities. I once had a girl tell me she wasn't mean; she was just honest. I wonder if she knew she was lying to herself. We all have insecurities, and they manifest in different ways. Right now, Lisa's insecurities are on display as she tries to intimidate the new girl and make her run away scared on her first day. What she doesn't know is that the things I'm insecure about make me double down and try harder. Maybe she'll surprise me and be a quick study.

I carefully close the case on my Kindle and look up at the trio, "I didn't realize elite schools came with waitstaff. I appreciate the dedication to your job, but I wasn't finished." I pull the tray back in front of me. I realize that choosing violence probably isn't the best tactic. Nevertheless, as previously mentioned, I can't show weakness either. Besides, the shade of red on Lisa's face is rivaling a chili pepper, and the image of her head as that chili pepper gives me a much-needed laugh. The twins standing on either side of her have mixed expressions, the one on the left of shock while the one on the right looks impressed.

"She has a backbone" the girl on the right says. "I like it." I get the sense that the girl on the right could be someone I'd like too, if only she hadn't aligned herself with what's shaping up to be the incarnation of entitlement.

"Not now Kate!" Lisa snaps. She needs to learn to treat her friends better. "Here's the deal, new girl. I'm willing to forgive your lapse in judgment for a moment. You haven't had time to learn the ropes. Clearly, not with your mentor being Ben." Interesting. She calls him Ben. "Fortunately for you, I volunteer to fill you in on the things he missed this morning."

"Isn't that sweet?" I deadpan. I hope my face portrays how unimpressed I am. I didn't expect Briarwood to live up to the stereotype of a typical private school so quickly. Snotty kids and all.

Lisa stills her face and continues, "Classes may be first come first serve, but it is well known that some students are served first."

"How classist of you" my comment doesn't break her stride.

"Families like mine helped build this school. Because of that, we get the first pick of classes for us and anyone we want in those classes. Now, Bella here can't take journalism with Kate because the new girl took the last spot." She pauses for effect. "See where I'm going with this?"

I stand and grab my bag off the floor, slipping my Kindle inside. I don't match her height, but I am sick of her towering over me. The intimidation tactics are old. "I see where you're going, so I'll stop you right there. I'm a journalism major; I was recruited by the school to do that. It's likely they expect me to take a class in, I don't know, journalism? Even if that wasn't the case, I'm not giving up my spot so you can have who I assume," I pause and nod to the twins, "are your only friends with you. Have a nice day. See you in class." I attempt to walk off. I should have figured that she wouldn't back down easily, as she quickly blocks my path. Apparently, she doesn't just look like a rabbit but is as fast as one. I wonder what sport she chose.

"Change majors." Is this girl serious? She is starting to draw attention. There goes all hope to fly under the radar.

"No. Now excuse me." I step around her and take off as quickly as I can to the door. It isn't time to meet Benedict yet, but maybe I can hunt down the library for a reprieve. No such luck. I hear little rabbit's footsteps behind me, accompanied by only what I can assume is the scurry of her minions. By the time I reach the door, I only have a second to take in my surroundings and choose a direction—either back toward the math wing or straight out to the courtyard. The image of dodging more of Mrs. Rollins' spit makes the decision for me. Courtyard it is.

Pushing through the heavy wooden door, the outside air greets me and so does the sight of Mr. Romcom himself in what looks like his own heated debate with Curly Q from earlier. Devil I know or entitled rabbit? I beeline for the couple, hoping he won't mind the interruption.

# Chapter 4

As I approach the couple, they are oblivious not only to me but also the collection of other students enthralled by their tiff. Beginning to second guess my decision, I get closer and hear the anger in the voice of the assumed flavor-of-the-week. "What do you mean you aren't coming? It's the first party of the year. Do you know how bad I'll look if you aren't there?" Maybe she isn't the flavor of the week, and he's an even bigger jerk than I suspected. Flirting with me when he has a girlfriend.

"Summer, I told you at the end of last year, I'm done. Done with you, done with the party scene, and now I'm done with this conversation." Or maybe I misjudged him after all. Now is the perfect time to announce myself.

"Sorry to interrupt this episode of "No Love Island", but Ben, I need help getting to my next class." They both turn to me. Benedict in shock and Summer with a look of disgust. You would think she swallowed a bug. She squeals at

Benedict, "Who the hell is this?". Calling him Ben instead of Benedict was calculating on my part. He looked like he needed saving, but I didn't think her reaction would be this intense. I bet this school has a killer drama program based on the reactions of the girls I've encountered so far. Benedict, quick to recover from his initial shock of my appearance leans into me. "Summer, this is my new friend, Amelia."

"Friend?" She scoffs. "Since when do you have friends that are girls?" She crosses her arms and shifts her weight onto one leg. Her pouty face makes me feel like I'm in a bad teen movie. I guess those films have to take inspiration from somewhere. I miss my small town. The girls were dramatic, yes, but not to this level. Plus, they were easier to avoid. Benedict shows no sympathy for her plight and is visibly annoyed by her tantrum.

"I started having friends that were girls when I stopped hanging out with the wrong girls." His voice carries a hint of venom, but he doesn't say it with as much determination as earlier. Still. Ouch. Summer looks like she might cry. "Let's go Amelia." Ben takes my bag and slings it over his shoulder, causing Summer to combust. He leads me to a door opposite of the way I came from. I follow along, feeling kind of bad for Summer. Yes, she is shrill, and a little rude, but it doesn't make rejection easier.

Rushing to keep pace with him, we go through another elegantly crafted wooden door. Benedict quickly pulls me by my arm into a small alcove nearby catching me completely off guard. The area houses a water bottle filling station and leaves little room for us to stand. His intention is clear as we are out of the line of sight of other students.

Craning my neck up to look at his face, I instantly regret interrupting him. His breathing is abnormal and makes his chest rise and fall, and the smirk that I assume is the reason he hasn't had many girls as friends has returned. "What? I'm Ben now?" I just stare. "Not that I mind. But didn't anyone ever tell you it's rude to interrupt?"

This guy. I narrow my eyes at him and ask, "Are you seriously scolding me for saving you?".

"Saving me?" He laughs, actually laughs. My cheeks heat. I'm not sure if it's out of embarrassment or anger. Probably a combination of both. "Dorothy, I didn't need saving from Summer."

Mimicking his tone I snap, "So now I'm back to Dorothy, huh? What happened to Amelia?" I bite back. "Besides, you could have fooled me." I contemplate my next words carefully. I had planned on flying under the radar this year. Focus on getting the education and experience I came for. Avoid making any unnecessary connections. However, after my scuffle with Lisa, having one friend might not be so bad. "Besides, it isn't bad manners when it's a friend." That dang smirk. He looks like he has won a prize. My insides coil. This is a bad idea. This space is too small.

"Okay. Amelia." His voice drops, and so does my stomach. This is a very bad idea. The tiny space leaves no room to back away. "Since we are friends now, we should probably get to know each other a little better."

My entire being is laced with uncertainty. The way he teases, trying to get a rise out of me. It's working, even though I wish it weren't. My god this space is small. Focus

Amelia! You have handled boys before. He is just a boy. Shut him down.

"What did you have in mind? Braiding each other's hair and gossiping about our love lives?" I question him. Sarcasm, my real best friend. Though I wouldn't mind getting my hands in his hair. Dang it Amelia. No.

"Sure." He matches my energy. "As long as we can have a pillow fight after."

"Let me guess, in our underwear?" I hope he can hear my eyes roll as well as see them. "Be more original."

"You brought it up, not me." He says, holding his hands up innocently. Ugh. I need out of this space and conversation but curiosity takes the lead.

"Let me guess. Summer is your ex?"

"Why so curious about Summer? Jealous?" He tries to sound flirty but is obviously building a wall.

"Just want to know if my tires are going to be slashed later." I don't know my own intention in asking honestly. The root of my curiosity couldn't possibly be jealousy. I've known this guy for five minutes.

"Summer is complicated. We didn't date per se. We have known each other for years and kind of hang out when it's convenient for each other." He chooses his words carefully. "She's upset that it's no longer convenient for me."

"Why?" the question slips and as soon as it does I'm desperate for the answer. Ben is an enigma. On the surface a clear party boy, but behind his eyes secrets brew.

"Enough about Summer." He pulls his phone out of his back pocket and checks the time. "We have to get you to class." He exits the alcove, leaving me no choice but to follow, again. As we step out of the little world we've created in the contained space, reality sets in and Ben shifts the conversation. "It's your turn to answer a question. Why the change in heart about being friends?"

I guess honesty is the best policy. "I ran into Lisa Taylor at lunch." I don't go into detail. Based on his expression, I won't have to.

"Damn, Dorothy, skipped the flying monkeys and met the Wicked Witch of the West." His tone is back to being playful. "Anyone would need a friend after that. Lisa thinks she runs the entire school. She's been the top of our class since kindergarten."

"You know her well?" We continue to walk down the maze of hallways. The structure of the school is overwhelming, navigating each day it going to be its' own complicated task. He wasn't kidding about my Lit class being a trek.

"Everyone knows Lisa, but yeah, I've known her longer than some. We've been in the same class since preschool.  Our families also have shared business ventures."

"Lucky you."

"Hardly." Something ticks in the corner of his eye. "I'd tell you not to worry about it, but I'm not surprised she tried to come for you. With your success in Journalism, she's threatened. Becoming editor of the school paper has been her dream since she could write a complete sentence. You threaten that with your stuff being picked up by the city paper."

"How do you know about that?" Did he research me? I'm hardly a famous author. I just had a couple of pieces I wrote for our local paper picked up.

"Google," he smirks. "Your stuff is good."

I'm surprised he read my articles. I've been working for the local gazette for years, fascinated with the way newspapers work since I was a kid. The editor took pity on me and let me volunteer in middle school, then I started freelancing. I helped get the paper digitalized and talked the editor into doing online posts. A couple of my pieces got picked up by City News. It's cool, but nothing a high school student would be interested in.

"You've read my articles?"

"Surprised Dorothy?" He stops for a moment.

"That you read. Yes." I know that I shouldn't tease when he's paying me a genuine compliment, but I'm uncomfortable under his praise.

"Ouch. You know I'm more than a pretty face, right?" He holds his hand to his heart in mock offense.

"I mean..." shrugging my shoulders.

"So, you agree. I have a pretty face?" he quips. Yup, walked right into that one.

"I just mean you seem like your interests would be directed in a different direction." I can't believe this is where this conversation has led.

"What type of direction?" He really doesn't want the answer to that.

"A Summer-shaped direction."

I can't pinpoint the emotion that plays out on his face. It isn't hurt or offended, but... pained.

"At one time you would've been right." His face drops.

"But not now?" I raise a brow and study his face. It's earnest.

"No, not now." I believe him.

"What changed?" I know it's too personal. Call it journalistic intrigue. I'm always after the story. At least that's what I am choosing to tell myself.

"We don't have time to answer that question. Besides, we're here." He points to a doorway. I still have questions, but I guess they'll have to wait.

"Any advice?" I can't explain it, even with the giant red flag and alarm bells going off in my mind, I feel comfortable with

Ben. He hasn't been boring, which can't be said for my past experiences with the guys at Wilcocks. I just hope I'm not being naïve again.

"Keep up with the reading. Even though I doubt that will be a problem for you." I wait for him to slip off my bag and hand it to me, but he doesn't. "After you?"

"You're coming in?" I thought he was a year older based on his mentor status. He couldn't have this class too.

"Obviously." He gestures for me to enter the room. All I hear is Professor Snape in my mind, but I will keep that tidbit of my personality hidden. We walk into the room, and I'm surprised to see there are no desks. There's one large round wooden table with cushioned leather chairs around it. It's more like a meeting area than a classroom. There's no teacher desk either, only a podium holding a laptop and a smart board. Ben takes my bag and sets it down closer to the board. We're the only students in the room. I sit down next to him and ask, "Are you sure we are in the right place?"

At the same time, a handsome man in his mid-thirties walks in. Mr. Laurence, I presume. He has dark brown hair that is combed back and is wearing a navy sweater, designer, with a light blue button-down underneath. Apparently, private school teachers get paid well. Does this school recruit all their teachers from a modeling company? I have to physically pick my jaw up. Suddenly I'm hyper-aware of Benedict staring at me staring at the teacher.

"Early birds. Glad to see some people are excited for the first day of school. Welcome back Mr. Blake. Who is your friend?" Has he taken one of his classes before?

"Mr. Laurence, this is Amelia Roberts. She's one of the new students from recruitment. I'm her mentor." His tone loses all playfulness and is serious. Even business-like.

"It's nice to meet you Miss Roberts. Welcome to Briarwood. I hope your first day has been successful so far?" His voice is warm. I can tell he actually means it when he says he hopes my first day is going well. Then his tone adjusts slightly with Ben "and Mr. Blake, it's good to see you taking your duties as a mentor seriously this year. I trust we can expect a new and improved Ben from last year?" Ben tenses next to me under Mr. Laurence's stern glare.

"Yes sir. New leaf" as if he doesn't believe himself, he adds "I promise." More students start to file in, and just like that, the exchange is over. I take out my notebook and favorite felt-tip pen. The headline for a news article scrolls across my mind. Who is Benedict Blake? Or better yet, who was he?

I stop myself. This isn't why I'm here. Do better Amelia.

# Chapter 5

As much as I hate calculus, I love American Lit. Mr. Laurance takes it far beyond the study of what some dead white guy has written. The classroom setup quickly made sense. According to Mr. Laurance, literature is meant to be discussed, not taught. His teaching style allows the students to take charge of the class. He acts only as a tour guide. This is the reason I'm here, the curriculum surpassing anything I would ever get at Wilcocks.

After the spit-diving Olympics of Calc and the soap opera-esque encounters with the *Girls of Briarwood Academy*, I finally have comfort in my decision to be here. When Mr. Laurance calls the class to a close, I don't want to leave. He does pass out a reading list about a mile long for our next class. Fortunately, most of it I have already read. I tore through our town library in elementary school. Then started spending any extra money I earned on creating my own personal library. The classics of American Literature are something I'm deeply familiar with.

I pack up my bag and attempt to sling it over my shoulder, but Ben has none of it. He takes both of our bags and leads me out of the room. Stepping back into the hall, a sense of relief washes over me. I finally take in my surroundings. The Literature Department spans over two T-shaped hallways. Within the halls, there are several small nooks that house large leather study chairs. I could make use of those. The walls, however, are lined with photos of alumni. All of whom have had success in the literary world. My eye catches on one photograph, and my heart swells. Roland Roberts. My grandfather. He owns the largest publishing house in Georgia with multiple companies under its' umbrella. Any of which with a phone call after graduation I could have my pick of. I won't though.

My mom and grandparents aren't on the best of terms. They aren't full no contact. However, beyond holiday dinners and cards on birthdays, the extent of the relationship ends. That is until recently. After my first article got picked up, I got a letter. An old-school letter with a wax seal and everything. It was from my grandfather. He told me how proud of me he was and asked if I wanted to have lunch. I didn't tell my mom. It felt like a betrayal. After all, I'm the reason for the falling out. It didn't stop me from going though. I went to the lunch and my grandfather was nothing like I expected.

My mom doesn't talk about her parents much. Just that she didn't want to rely on their money, and she didn't. She worked from the minute she left home at 19 with 1-year-old me. She got a job as a night manager at a bed and breakfast. Renting out a room from the owner, Mrs. Pat. When the owner wanted to retire, they worked out a payment plan for my mom to buy the place. The thing about mom is that she is truly brilliant.

She barely missed graduating from Briarwood. It was close to the beginning of her senior year when she got pregnant and she hid it until she couldn't anymore. My grandparents homeschooled her when they found out. She still got her high school diploma and attended classes at the local college to get a bachelor's in hospitality. I think my grandfather is secretly proud of her too. I just wish he would reach out and tell her. I would never tell my mom, but I crave some sort of father figure.

Mine took off when my mom refused to marry him after she got pregnant. He doesn't try to have a relationship so why should I? My grandfather, on the other hand, at least he is making an attempt.

"Thinking of getting a copy for your wall? Won't it clash with your boy band posters?" Ben's comment breaks me from my thoughts.

"Do I really look like I have boy band posters?" I look up at him expectantly. He grins a full-on grin, no smirk.

"I mean I could come over after school and find out?" We start walking down the hall.

"It is after school." I'm still a little off from finding the photograph of my grandfather, not thinking of the ramifications of my response.

"Great! You drive. I'm too tired from carrying your bag around." I know he isn't serious, but the constant flirtation in his voice causes me to toe a line I'm not comfortable with.

"A. I didn't ask you to take my bag and B. I'm not driving you anywhere. I'm going home to get started on the Calc homework and finish an article I started for the gazette." I'm also going home to study the campus map, tear through the online portal for all my classes, and get a head start on my assignments for Anatomy and Journalism. He doesn't need to know that when it comes to school, I can be overly obsessive. I just want to do well here.

"The Windy Creek Gazette?" I'm shocked he knows the name of my hometown paper, although I shouldn't be if he read my articles. The paper has always been cited when my articles are republished.

"Yes. Why?" I ask hesitantly.

"I guess I'm just surprised the Briarwood Messenger would let you double up." I honestly hadn't considered it. I've been allowed free rein for so long at the gazette that the thought of a conflict never crossed my mind. The messenger mostly reports on school events with the option for featured pieces. The benefit of their program is that it will give me experience in all aspects of running a paper. Some more modern training than anything I could ever get at the gazette. Also, at the end of the year, a senior editor will be picked. I need that on my resume for college.

"I guess I'll find out tomorrow."

At this point, we've approached the student parking lot. The lot is filled with expensive cars, Porsche's, BMWs, Range Rovers. I felt uncomfortable pulling in, but my nerves of finding the admissions office and getting my schedule won out. Now that Ben is still walking with me, I'm feeling slightly insecure. I hate that. I knew going into this the kids here would have more money than me but letting them silently judge me is better than my status being right in the only person I know face.

"Well, thanks for getting me around today, but I have to be going." I reach for my bag, but he refuses.

"Hold it Dorothy. I told you before, I cannot in good conscience let you carry this bag. I'll walk you to your car."

"No, it's fine. Really. I've got it." I make for the bag again. He still pulls back.

"Dorothy" he drags out "What's going on? I thought we had made it to friendship?" Ugh.

"I don't want you to see my car, okay. I'm embarrassed." I mean my car isn't anything embarrassing to the normal eye. I actually love it. It's my mom's old jeep. She upgraded recently and it was perfect timing seeing how I have a 30-minute commute to Briarwood. I love the faded blue and even the collection of decals my mom added. I just. It doesn't fit here, which points out the more significant issue that I don't fit. Which is stupid, I know. They recruited me. Chose me. Given I had an advantage over other recruits because of my family name. I just didn't have the funds to back it up.

"Listen Amelia, all jokes aside, you don't have to be embarrassed by what you drive. Some kids here may be entitled and think that their money makes them better than everyone else, but you can exclude me from that list."

The response was more serious than anything he has said to me by far, leaving me unsure how to handle it.

"Thanks," is all I have in me.

"Now come on." More and more students start to pile out of the buildings into the parking lot. "We don't want you getting swept up in a tornado." I wonder what his obsession with The Wizard of Oz is. Nevertheless, I don't argue and start walking toward the back of the lot to my Jeep. The parking lot quickly turns into chaos. Students everywhere pulling off ties and blazers. Groups start to form at cars laughing and talking. Some kids walk with their faces in their phone screens. Briarwood has a strict no-phone-use policy in class or hallways. You can have one, just not be actively using it. According to the handbook, the policy is enforced heavily.

As we continue the walk to the far back row where I parked, I start to notice several people looking in our direction as we pass. Ben waves at a couple people. Apparently, he has a level of popularity.

When we reach my jeep, I realize I can't unlock it because Ben has my bag, with my key. "Thanks for walking me, but I need my bag back, it has my key." He finally hands me back my bag, the weight catching me off guard. It's heavier than I remember. I see a smile tug at the corner of Ben's lips to say I told you so. I choose to ignore it and retrieve my car key from the front pocket. I slide the key into the door and turn it twice to unlock all four doors. The clicker stopped working years ago.

I open the back door and throw my book bag into the back seat. It makes a thud that shakes the car a little. Maybe I could lighten the load. Shutting the car door, I turn to face Ben who is doing a sweep of the lot with his eyes. I take advantage of his distraction and get a better look at his face. He really does look like he could be from a romantic comedy. I hate to admit it, but if I were a different girl, I'd happily be in that movie with him. Play the part of the brainy and nerdy love interest. This, however, is not a movie and I'm not a different girl. His eyes finish their sweep and stare right back into mine.

"Thanks for your help today." Uncomfortable holding eye contact, I turn to get into my car. "See you tomorrow?" It's a question I know the answer to. As my mentor, it's his job to get me to my classes tomorrow too. His job. Keep reminding yourself of that, Amelia.

"You're welcome Amelia. Yeah tomorrow. Drive safe." No taunt. No Smirk. Just a small smile.

"Bye Ben." I get into my car, and he walks away toward a group of boys. I take a moment and watch him interact. Then I shake it off and start my car. It's time to leave the walls of great expectation and return to the comfort of my small town. My phone connects automatically to the speaker, an upgrade I was happy to make to the outdated Jeep. I start the audio version of the book I was so rudely interrupted reading during lunch. Ugh. Lisa. That will be tomorrow's problem. For now, I have 30 minutes to escape into a fantasy world.

**Benedict's point of view**

This school year was going to suck. After my suspension last year, returning on the condition that I join the mentor program left me in a foul mood. But I had it coming. I spiraled out of control at the end of last year, culminating in that idiotic break-in of the headmaster's office. I'm lucky I wasn't expelled. Dad pulled out all the stops to keep me here, even playing the sick mom card.

One more screw-up and it's off to boarding school. Dad doesn't make empty threats. And I can't afford to screw up now, not with Mom in such critical condition. I owe it to her to get my act together. I didn't realize then how much the cancer had taken a toll on her. So I accepted my punishment without hesitation.

I thought I'd be paired with some clueless freshman I could easily shuttle around and ignore. Boy, was I wrong.

I got her file a week ago. She's a new recruit for the Journalism program, but I already knew who she was even before I got the official dossier. The elusive granddaughter of Roland Roberts. She probably doesn't know our grandfathers are friends. When Dad mentioned I'd be part of the mentor program, they set the whole thing up. I'd never seen her until today, but I did my research and found her articles online. She's got an impressive style.

It wasn't until I saw her in the hallway that I realized how stunning she is. Flirting was instinctive, but it was her immediate shutdown that really intrigued me. It's never happened to me before. She's assertive and bold, yet there's something innocent in those big blue eyes that makes me want to protect her. I know firsthand how cutthroat this school can be, especially with the girls. That's what led me to the admissions office.

"Hey Rose" I say with a smile, knowing it'll work its charm. She startles at the sight of me, then stumbles over her words.

"Um, hi, Ben, I mean Benedict. What can I help you with?"

I lean in closer. "I need help with my schedule. I need it to match this." I slide Amelia's schedule across the counter to her. She takes it, then smiles.

"I can't enroll you in calc again, Ben, but there's an opening in the Journalism class. Lisa scared someone out of it hoping Bella could have the spot. But oh darn. It's filled now." She starts typing away. I like Rose. She's quiet but has a devious side. She knows everyone's secrets but only spills them for the right price.

"Anatomy is no problem; I can switch it out since you were going to have it next semester anyway. And you're already signed up for Golf as a teacher's assistant in the afternoon section, but I can switch you to mornings. Barkley needs an assistant since Peterson dropped."

"Perfect" I say. I plan to be a very good mentor. "Thanks for the help."

"Anytime, Ben, but one thing," she adds.

"Yeah?" I pause before heading out.

"Amelia is a nice girl," she warns.

"I know. Later Rose."

As far as anyone knows, I'm doing her grandfather a favor, keeping an eye out for her. But this is all for me. This year isn't going to suck so bad after all.

# Chapter 6

Sitting on my bed in the middle of my room, I fidget with a ruffle on my light pink comforter as I read through the syllabus for Anatomy. The class is set up simple enough. It's broken down in a combination of lectures and labs. The final counts for 50% of my grade. That doesn't make me want to vomit at all. I lay back for a moment and take a breath looking around my room.

My room has always been my comfort zone. The walls are lined with bookshelves that my mom's friend Jacob built for me. He owns the local hardware store and helped Mom renovate the inn when she bought it. My room was included in that renovation. I have strategically filled them over the years. As one reached capacity, Jacob would build another. He jokes that he'll have to put bookshelves under my bed at this point, but I love it. It's like sleeping in a library. My own carefully curated library.

I have all the classics, history books, books on special interests, and even some of my favorite children's books. One shelf is dedicated fully to fantasy. The shelves don't only hold books. They also hold photographs of me, my mom, a few of me and Sarah Mae. There are some academic awards littered around too and small figurines from different fantasy novels I love.

As a journalist I write about the real world and call attention to problems in a new light, however, when escaping to my room isn't enough, going into another world is just the fix. Unfortunately, there is no escaping the feeling that I'm in over my head.

I have read over the course description and syllabus for my Journalism class five times. The class is completely immersive. The school publishes a physical paper each week, as well as daily blog posts. Competitive doesn't even begin to cover it. My stomach growls, reminding me that I do actually have to leave my room at some point tonight.

Mom should be finished up with the nighttime rounds by now. The thing about living at the inn you run is that you're never really off the clock. It made for an interesting childhood. I got to meet people from all over, but it also makes for lack of privacy. Our apartment is separated from the guests' rooms with our own private living area, and mom hires a weekend manager, so she has time off, but still. I can't just go sit outside without the possibility of running into guests. I groan and lift off the bed. When I finally work up enough nerve to leave my sanctuary and enter our living room, I see my mom off the open floor plan in the kitchen area.

Mom is gorgeous in her own right. She is tall whereas I am short. She has long brown hair that always sits perfectly where I have blonde wavy hair that I have to put too much product in just to get it to behave. The Georgia humidity is no friend of mine. The only thing identical about us is our eyes. We both have bright blue eyes.

As I approach the kitchenette, I notice that she has a tray filled with all my favorite junk foods. Pizza bagels, tater tots, taquitos, and even a soft pretzel with cheese. So much for a nutritious dinner. If Gabriel the in-house chef saw this collection he would die, come back to life, and then immediately make me eat a pan-seared pork chop with honey-roasted green beans. There's a reason my mom had to outsource that particular job. I smile. She looks up at me and says in her Smeagol voice, "The study troll has emerged, must feed it substance, so it doesn't smash the village." I just laugh.

"Really, mom? I'm not that bad."

Moving with the tray to the coffee table she plops down on our faded blue sofa. At one time it was a bright royal blue, but no longer. The sofa, I'm pretty sure is older than me but is the most comfortable seat in the entire inn. "You've been locked in your room since you got home. I barely got two sentences from you before you came up."

"I'm sorry, I just had a lot of homework."

She gives me a pointed look. "On the first day? Is this homework assigned by the teacher or by Amelia to get ahead?"

"Both?" I laugh. "Am I really that bad?"

"Honey, you snuck your books home in first grade and completed an entire 9 weeks of work over a weekend." She is teasing but there's pride in her eyes. "I should have put you in a private school then, I just didn't" She drifts off. She gets the same sad look she has every time we pull into my grandparents' house. A combination of regret and longing.

"I know. You didn't want me in that world." I grab a pizza bagel off the tray and lay my head in her lap. "After today I can see why."

She strokes my hair. "Bad first day?"

It takes time to formulate a response. I guess it isn't all bad. I don't want her to worry and think that she made a mistake pushing me to go. I don't think mentioning my mentor situation is a good idea either. Boys are a sore subject. My mom isn't anti-dating, she's just anti-distraction. My one and only attempt at having a boyfriend didn't end well. She's still bitter from when I told her the reason for my breakup with the seemingly perfect small town guy. I don't keep secrets from her, generally, excluding one aforementioned letter from my grandfather. She knows all the details as to why I ended my relationship with Tyler. As it turns out, small-town boys don't match up with big dreams.

"Not bad, just different." I pause. "Intense." For a writer, I sure am struggling with words today.

"Intense how?" I figured that answer wouldn't suffice. I come by my inquisitive nature honestly. I was left with no choice but to spill about the encounter with Lisa. I also mentioned that my mentor was male. I didn't go into detail about his flirtatious nature or that I had let my determination of a distraction-free year waiver after only one class. On the bright side, her upset with Lisa distracted her from any questions about Ben.

We spent the rest of the night tearing through the tray of snacks. Mom talked me into staying out of my room long enough for an episode of Golden Girls, our go-to comfort show. After promising not to stay up too late reading through my course materials, I closed myself off in my room.

Back in my sanctuary, I send Sarah Mae a text promising to fill her in over the weekend of all the "Briar patch" as she calls it, tea. Having a best friend that gets I need to focus this week is the best. Even if I do feel like I abandoned her. She has been my rock.

Besides, she has her art friends to keep her occupied. Sarah Mae is one of the most talented artists I have ever met. She lives and breathes her work. While she specializes in painting, she has recently undertaken working with clay and has been known to go into a hole for days working on a piece. It's why we work well together. The ability to be in a room for hours not speaking while she paints, and I read or work on my latest piece.

Finally ready to settle down for the night, I change into my pajamas. I suppose pajamas are a loose term. NYU sweatshirt and shorts. I've wanted to go to NYU since my mom and I took a trip to New York when I was 10. I fell in love with the city. A night owl, the idea of being in a city that never sleeps is more than appealing. It's a love my mom and I share.

The only story she tells me about her childhood is when my grandfather took her to see her first Broadway play. The nanny had quit, and he was forced to take her on a business trip. The way she painted the city her eyes brightened. She said she knew she had to take me one day.

Despite having to fight the anxiety that comes with me moving far away, she's always encouraged my big ambitions. She sees the way I come to life in the city. Don't get me wrong, I love my small town, but I want to experience more than the corn husking festival and spring jubilee.

Laying in my bed staring up at the ceiling, I struggle to fall asleep under the uncertainty of what tomorrow brings. Usually, the first week of school I'm glowing with excitement, and I am about the classes. I just feel like finding my way around socially will be an educational experience in itself.

Eventually, I fall into a fitful sleep. Complete darkness encases me then a soft glow emerges. The thorns from the Briarwood emblem begin to wrap around my body slowly. I fight against them and as a struggle the thorns consume me. My breathing becomes jagged. This is the same dream I've had every night for the last week. Something is different this time, I can see a fuzzy shape emerging out of the darkness. Then a voice drowns out my ragged breath. "Don't worry Dorothy, I got you." Ben?

The drive to school this morning gave me enough time to formulate a plan for the day. Well, a plan and a list of rules.

**Rules:**

1. Do not engage in banter with Ben. It doesn't matter how funny and witty he is, or how good his hair looks. Do not engage.
2. Avoid conflict with Lisa. Focus on getting an article picked for the first edition of the paper.
3. Keep your head down and get the education you came for.

A simple set of rules to reset my focus and make sure I don't get off track. I'll apply the first pancake theory to yesterday. Of course, my first day was bound to have a funky shape. So, toss it out and make today better. To start, accept that I don't need all the books in the world in my backpack. I can get by with my notebooks, laptop, and Kindle. If I have the locker, I should use it. This way, Ben can't find any reason to "have to" carry my bag.

It's getting close to time for my first class and no sight of Ben in the hall. Looking around there's nothing but rows of blue lockers and students shuffling around the hall. There seems to be more traffic than yesterday, but that may just be because I was distracted. I did manage to print a campus map out and mark the location and best routes to all my classes. Pulling it out of my bag and closing my locker I locate my route. I even put a star on the location of my locker. The Journalism room is off the English wing and shouldn't be too hard to find on my own.

I end up finding the classroom easily. Peeking in the doorway, to my surprise Ben is sitting at a table near the front of the room on a laptop. Behind him, Lisa is staring daggers into the back of his head with Kate or Bella next to her. I'm not sure which one. Hesitating and taking a breath, I enter the room.

The setup reminds me of the circulation room at the Gazette. Six large tables in the middle of the room with laptop plug-in stations. A wall of computers next to the door. On the opposite side, there are large glass windows looking out onto a small courtyard. The back of the room holds a large machine, which I assume is used for printing. Anticipation buzzes at my fingers. Despite my initial nerves. This is home. The smell of ink in the air electrifies my senses.

Ben's face looks up from his laptop as I walk deeper into the room; he smiles. Rules, Amelia, you have rules. I nod my head, politely smile back then sit at the table opposite the side of the room but aligned with his. I'm not risking getting close to Lisa. I am not afraid; I just want to avoid any

50

confrontation. It's not the same thing. I have rules, remember.

With my back now to Ben, Lisa, and unidentified twin, I take out my supplies. I managed to draft two articles last night, so I power my laptop on and get them pulled up and ready. Based on my research of the paper, the back-to-school edition always includes a spotlight section for featured articles. I want one of those spots. Movement next to me causes my attention to shift, I turn in the direction to see Ben. He's not impressed. Setting a coffee holder on the table with two cups in it and resting one hand on the table, he leans over me, invading my space. Rules, Rules, Rules! My god he smells good. Like coffee and cologne. Not the cheap body spray that haunts the halls of Wilcocks, but something different. Expensive. Musky. Leather mixed with citrus, then combined with the coffee, it should disgust me, however… NO, Amelia. Rules!

"Good morning, Amelia. Did you not like the seats I picked for us? I got here early for them." His voice is huskier than usual. Is he messing with me?

"Good morning, you didn't have to save me a seat," I have to force the politeness, so it doesn't come off as rude or flirty. "I'm sure that you probably have friends you want to sit with. I'll be okay."

He isn't having it. He sits down right next to me and hands me a cup of coffee. I take it on instinct despite the fact that I already drank a cup on the way here. I know. I know. Coffee stunts your growth, but it's too late for me. "Thank you," I stare into his eyes, a big mistake. The blue from yesterday is a stormy gray today.

"Now what kind of a mentor would I be if I left you alone," he smirks at me as I sip the coffee. It's the perfect ratio of cream and sugar. I hold back a moan. His voice drops to more of a whisper, "Besides, I heard Lisa is homicidal after the last seat of the class was snatched up."

This is not news to me; from her accosting me yesterday, I already knew today might end up a hot mess. "I think I got that memo yesterday." Then it hits me. "Hey, why didn't you tell me we have Journalism together?"

He sips his coffee and shrugs his shoulders, "Didn't come up?" He isn't wrong. I didn't exactly ask for his life story. Out loud anyway.

"Do we have any other classes together?" I should be prepared if I'm going to have to spend all day with him. I need to formulate some new rules.

"Anatomy and Golf" he shrugs.

"So, everything but calculus." I raise a brow at him. The one class I might actually need help in. "I thought you were a year ahead of me."

"I never said that." He responds nonchalantly.

"I just assumed because you were my mentor you would be older." It would make sense.

"Not how it works, Dorothy," the "*We aren't in Kansas anymore*", goes without saying. I turn back to my computer as more students file in the room. Finally, the teacher walks in.

Mr. Bannerman is short and stout. My theory that all the teachers in the school are recruited from a modeling agency is immediately dismantled. He looks like a cartoon character from a newspaper office. He even has the stereotypical mustache. I half expect him to pull a cigar out at any moment.

When he opens his mouth, it doesn't get better. With a thick Boston accent, he addresses the class. "Welcome back, everyone. I trust you all had productive summers full of internships, travels, and a limited number of shenanigans." I have to hide the smile that threatens to bloom. In the corner of my eye, I see Ben watching my reaction. I fix my face. He continues, "I see we have some new faces this year." My face floods with heat. Please don't introduce me, please don't introduce me. Please don't be that guy. "I want to welcome Amelia Roberts to our staff. She comes to us from the small town of Windy Creek. We are happy to have you with us. I enjoyed your article recently published in City News about how social media is a sleight of hand distraction from current events. Insightful stuff."

I have to clear my voice, "Thank you, sir." I leave out the last part thanking him for putting a big target on my back.

He continues, "Mr. Blake, welcome to our ranks as well. I look forward to seeing what you have to offer us this year."

I momentarily pause my own mortification. Was Ben not in journalism before? I turn to look at him, but his eyes are trained forward. "Thank you for having me, Mr. Bannerman. I look forward to being on staff."

Mr. Bannerman continues to spit out a few more introductions, but the questions are turning in my mind. In the span of 1 minute, I have run several interviews with Ben in my mind, none of which explain why he is in this class, other than me. Which is crazy. Why would he take a class for a girl he met yesterday? It has to be a coincidence. Right?

There's no ceremonial passing of the syllabus. No lecture. As it turns out, the class is already an established unit. Mr. Bannerman gave a few simple instructions, then the room shifts into action. People align themselves into stations and begin working. I feel lost and don't know where to go. I look to Ben for guidance, but he is relaxed in his seat looking unbothered.

"Roberts, Blake, come here!" Bannerman's voice stirs me out of my panic, and I cross the room quickly. Ben follows me in a comfortable stride. Curse his long legs. Must be nice.

"Sir," I address Mr. Bannerman.

"Here is the deal, most of the staff have established positions. We assigned beats at the end of last school year and won't reevaluate until after the first edition is published." My heart sinks. If everything is assigned, what am I even doing here? "Fortunately, for you Ben, our sportswriter, Peterson dropped the class at the last minute. I take it you can handle writing up a piece covering summer sports and what is upcoming in the fall. Highlight some of the senior athletes?"

"Actually, sir, Amelia has been dying to cover sports. She was telling me before class how she can't wait to get into the press box." Has he lost his mind?

"No, I—" I begin to protest, then Ben starts laughing.

"Keep your jokes to yourself, son." Bannerman scolds.

"Sorry sir. Had to." he straightens. "I can cover sports no problem. I assume I'll be sharing the beat with James?" Again, how is he this comfortable with teachers?

"You assume correct, get to work." Ben scurries off, leaving me alone and with no support. Some mentor he is.

"Now, Miss Roberts, you are a rarity. The recruiting efforts are newly formed and didn't align with the creation of new spots on staff," he says matter-of-factly. "However, I meant what I said about your writing. I've also spoken with the editor of your local paper, and he assures me that you are a prodigy. Combine that with your talent, I'm giving you features. You'll have to share the space with some of our other talented writers, but I trust you'll have no struggles."

"Thank you, sir." What else am I supposed to say? "I've actually already prepared a couple of articles for the first edition."

"Living up to your reputation already," he nods, "very good. Go ahead and take a table and finish off editing your pieces. Have three options ready to submit by the end of class."

"Right away." I move back to my laptop.

"Oh, and I'll send a student over in a bit to show you around the circulation area and get you familiarized with the space." Please don't be Lisa.

"Thank you." Once I resettle in my seat, I attempt to immerse myself in my articles, but I can't help but steal a glance at the room. To my dismay, Mr. Bannerman makes his way over to Lisa and the unidentified twins' table. As he talks with his back to me, I see her nod then scowl. She looks in my direction, murder in her eyes. Twin says something, and she turns to her, shocked, and shakes her head. I look away, hoping my assumptions are wrong and pour myself into my first article. It's a piece detailing the new recruiting initiative. Spot-on, but I'm hoping as a recruit I can offer a fresh perspective that the otherwise entitled student may not have. Go big or go home. Hopefully the former.

I manage to successfully shut out the world for a full 30 minutes before I feel a presence rather than see it.

I look up to see the unidentified twin standing in front of me with an amused look on her face. "Hi, I don't think we got to formally meet yesterday. I'm Kate."

"Amelia," I let out unsurely.

"I know." She smiles. "Mr. Bannerman asked me to show you around. Actually, he asked Lisa, but I thought letting her implode on our first day back in circulation would be bad for her skin."

"Okay, thanks, I guess."

"No problem, Bedelia, let's get started. Up, up." She actually claps her hands at me. I would have a smart retort if I didn't want to get this over. She is, after all, the lesser of all evil at this point. Standing, I can't let it fully go. "It's Amelia."

"I know, Amelia Bedelia. Now come on." I stare at her aghast. She is elegantly pretty and has a relaxed posture while still carrying herself with confidence.

"Right, where do we start?" I straighten myself.

Apparently, her confidence is earned. She knows the layout and mechanisms of the paper intricately. As we move around the room, the other students stop their work to regard her. It isn't the same reaction Lisa has. With Lisa, the other students wince out of her way. Kate smiles and is… friendly. It makes me wonder how she is friends with someone as entitled as Lisa. Despite my fading disdain for her by association, I remind myself she is still the competition. I can't let my guard down.

After we complete a lap around the room, we end up back at my original table. Before I can return to my chair, Kate grabs my arm, looks around, and then whispers, "One more thing. What's the deal with you and Ben?"

I look over her shoulder in his direction at the table. He has headphones in and is completely plugged into his laptop. What is the deal with Ben?

"He's my mentor." It is the only fact I'm sure of. "Why?"

"I've known him since kindergarten, and I have never seen him go out of his way for a girl before. He's more of a whatever falls into his lap kind of a guy. Then he takes the last spot in the class and warns Lisa to back off you. That doesn't really scream, mentor only." He did what!?! I knew it was strange he didn't mention being in any of my classes yesterday. What the hell. Of course, my stupid face displays every thought for Kate to read. "I take it you didn't know that. Really interesting."

"Nothing of interest here." There has to be a rational answer. "I'm sure he's just being a good mentor. I mentioned the conversation from the lunchroom. That must be it."

"Maybe, but I doubt it. New girl thing aside, you don't seem naive to me." She checks her surroundings again before continuing. "Listen, I don't share Lisa's contentment for opening the school up. I don't want anyone to fail here. I'll deny it if you repeat that. However, I should warn you, Ben doesn't have a good track record here. He almost got kicked out last year, but his dad made some sort of deal with the headmaster. Just be careful." The warning is sincere. I had already figured getting involved with Ben would be nothing but a distraction, but this is all the information I need to solidify my decision.

"Thanks for the concern, but it isn't needed. He is just my mentor." She shrugs and walks off.

Now I just have to calculate my next move. Not wanting to give up any more time working on my article, I put a pin in the Ben thing. For now. I fully plan to confront him, but now is not the time.

# Chapter 8

I end up working through lunch, and it seems that I'm not the only one. The journalism room is still half full. My three submissions are ready. I put my heart into the recruiting piece but have the other two to fall back on. I submitted them via the online paper portal and saved them to my computer drive and online drive. I prefer the "save it in at least three places" approach to writing. It took only one time losing a paper I worked on for days to adopt it.

Unfortunately, I won't know if my article gets selected until the edition comes out. Seniors do all the formatting. According to Kate, junior editors won't be picked until after winter break. There are only two spots for junior editors and the week before selection is hell week. Tensions get high; I can't wait. The one area I have never lacked confidence in is my writing.

I leave the journalism room in a buzz. Based on my map, the science building is across the courtyard. If I rush, I can avoid

Ben and get there on my own. He is caught in a deep conversation with Mr. Bannerman. While I really do want to confront him, how will that conversation go? "Hey, are you stalking me? According to the girl I have also only known for a day, you took the last spot in the journalism class, which is weird because I thought I had taken the last spot."

I make it halfway across the courtyard before the shuffle of rushed feet sound behind me. Wonder who that is? Picking up my pace a disheveled Ben blocks my path. I look up to see his shirt has wrinkled and come untucked a little. He is a tad out of breath. "Avoiding me, Dorothy?" he huffs.

"No, I just don't want to be late for Anatomy." I walk around him, and he blocks my path again. "Problem, Benedict?" It was naive of me to think I could avoid him. Better to get this sorted now than drag it out over the course of the week.

"Benedict? Thought we were past that." He slips his hand into his pockets, looking innocent and it's annoying. He can't possibly be hurt. I wouldn't be surprised if I'm just a game to him. Well, I'm not playing.

"Did you switch into Journalism because I was taking it?" His face levels. Busted. He is some sort of private school stalker.

"I did," he drags his hand through his hair. One hand is still in his pocket. His shoulders tense. He shouldn't be so handsome right now. "I asked to have some of my classes shifted to match yours."

I wasn't expecting honesty. If he is a stalker, he isn't doing a good job. Caught off guard, I stare at him in expectation.

"Look, I am going to tell you something, but you aren't going to like it."

"Continue," I gesture with my hand.

"I wasn't randomly assigned as your mentor. My father set it up with your grandfather. He wanted to make sure you got off to a good start." He knows my grandfather. I'm a family favor. My brain feels like the load screen on an old school computer, stuck on a processing page. "At first, I figured I would just show you around to your classes and make sure you got around okay, then you told me about the lunchroom with Lisa—"

"And you decided to go full stalker?" It's one thing that my grandfather is meddling. I'm not too mad because I'm sure it comes from a place of caring, but switching into my classes is outlandish. I could handle Lisa on my own.

"It sounds creepy when you say it like that." He attempts at defending himself.

"It is creepy. Favor or no favor, changing your schedule to match mine is absurd." I'm almost shouting. I lower my voice to avoid attracting attention.

"My intentions aren't creepy, I promise. I've known Lisa for years. I knew she wouldn't back off you, so I switched into the Journalism class so she couldn't mess with you." He explains. Am I supposed to believe he some sort of knight in shining blazer?

"And my other classes, did we share those too? Or did you transfer into those?" Guilty again.

"I transferred, but I promise it's only so I can keep an eye out for you." He has to know that is something the serial killer says in a scary movie. My face gives me away and he attempts to explain further. "Not like that, think of it as a big brother protective, well not brother. I don't want you to think of me as a brother. Shit. I'm not explaining this right." He is more and more flustered, and it's kind of cute. No, Amelia, stalkers aren't cute.

"I'm not a princess. I don't need protection. It's a school. Transfer out of my classes." He is smiling down at me. Psycho.

"No can do Dorothy. You may not be a princess, but you do need protection. I promised to look out for you, and that is what I am going to do. Now come on, we are going to be late." I only start walking again because I don't want to be late for class, not because he said so. I'm also not sitting next to him in class.

"Quit calling me Dorothy." I am full-on pouting. I'm not sure which one bothers me more at this point. That he thinks I am some damsel in need of a bodyguard or that I'm a favor. I choose not to mull it over too hard. I guess it helps me either way. If I am just a favor, his flirtation isn't real, and I don't have to worry about him being a distraction.

"Okay, princess." ugh.

"Not that either." I scold.

"Then what would you like me to call you?"

"Amelia."

"No, I think I'll stick to Dorothy."

"Ass."

**Benedict**

She can hurl insults at me all she wants, but I'm not budging from her classes. Admittedly, I may come across as a bit of a creep, but it's a label I'll bear if it means keeping her safe. Leaving her alone with Lisa and her clique was a recipe for disaster. What Amelia doesn't realize is that even in the confines of high school, there are still lurking dangers. I should know; I used to be one. That's the old me. I wouldn't dream of taking advantage of her now.

There's an innocence about Amelia that's both captivating and concerning. She's smart, witty, and undeniably attractive, but her confidence might land her in hot water. I've witnessed firsthand how ruthless Lisa can be, and I shudder to think what she'll do with Amelia as competition. My presence offers her some protection, a shield against the storm. I can't protect her if I'm not there. Sure, I could have transferred into the Journalism class alone, but that wouldn't cut it.

Golf. She signed up for Golf. Coincidentally enough, I have grown up on the golf course, which is why I take it every year to fill a credit, and I have seen what happens when I girl signs up. The thought of other guys in that class hovering around her, offering unsolicited advice—or God forbid correcting her form— it's enough to make my blood boil. Amelia may not grasp her allure as the new girl, but mark my words: she'll become a shiny new toy for every guy in sight. A trophy to be won.

I don't want to collect Amelia like some prize on a shelf. I want to know her, to understand her. It's a desire I've never felt before. Sure, I'll probably mess things up along the way. Yes, transferring into all her classes may have been a mistake, but I'm not backing down now. Besides, there was something endearing about her scolding me. She may be small in stature, but her fiery spirit is impossible to ignore. Deep down, she knows I'm right.

# Chapter 9

Ben was right. Dang it. Lisa is in my Anatomy class too, with BOTH twins. I had no choice but to let him be my lab partner. He may be giving stalker vibes for transferring into my class, but she gives murder vibes. Reunited with Bella, Lisa is worse than before. Silver lining, I can tell the twins apart now. Kate's hair flows freely while Bella's is pulled back into a tight ponytail. Bella hovers close to Lisa at all times and is perpetually, tense while Kate is at ease moving about talking and laughing with her lab partner, a scrawny kid that only takes his eyes off her to look into his microscope. The entire class, I feel Lisa's eyes on me.

When the bell finally rings, I yearn for a moment of respite. Unlike Calc, the coursework wasn't overly challenging, especially after reading ahead. I simply crave escape from all the drama, longing to retreat back to my small town. There is no place like home. I know, I heard it. The Dorothy thing is getting to me.

Before I can make my way back to Kansas, I need to swing by my locker to grab some books. I groan at the thought of trekking all the way across campus again but shuffle down the hall anyway. Ben insists on walking with me, taking on the role of my personal secret service. If that's what he wants, I'll oblige, keeping conversation to a minimum.

Arriving at my locker, I find it blocked by Lisa, arms crossed and scowling. How did she get here so fast? Kate leans nearby appearing bored, while Bella mirrors Lisa's posture. I inwardly curse, realizing Ben probably feels justified in his protective stance. He moves ahead, evidently ready to confront Lisa, but I step forward, unwilling to let him speak for me. Pushing past him, I stand directly in front of Lisa, meeting her gaze. Forget my previous rules; they hadn't worked with Ben, after all.

"Did the school hire locker attendants now? With all these side jobs Lisa, how do you manage your classes?" I quip, feigning innocence. Kate snickers, deepening the furrow in Lisa's brow.

"I wouldn't mouth off if I were you, new girl. I was being nice yesterday, but I'm not feeling as kind today." Lisa snips, embodying the mean girl high school cliche.

"Oh no, just when I thought I was going to be invited to a back-to-school slumber party." I reply pretending to pout.

"Keep it up, this is your last warning. Transfer back to whatever podunk town you came from." Lisa threatens. Ben tenses beside me, but remains silent.

"No thanks, I'm good. I'd miss our chats too much," I coo sweetly. "Now, if there's nothing else. I need to get to my locker. I wouldn't want to be late for butter churning." I maintain a composed demeanor, refusing to let her small-town jabs rattle me.

Suddenly Lisa invades my space. In an instant, Kate moves forward in case Lisa needs to be pulled back, and Ben stiffens, but before anyone can get to her, she lowers her voice and menacingly says, "Is that what your mom is doing now? Huh? Churning butter for money? Probably all she can do after dropping out to have you. Like mother, like daughter. You already have Benedict wrapped around your finger, trailing after you. Wonder why that is." The red haze of anger clouds my vision as I instinctively shove her away. But before I could do more, an arm wraps around me, pulling me back. I've never pushed anyone before, never been this angry. Looking forward I see Lisa with a smile on her face.

"What the hell, Lisa?" Kate snaps, stepping forward.

"What? I didn't say anything that wasn't true." Lisa shoots back, taking on a smug stance. The anger continues to course over me and a fight against Ben's grasp.

"No, you know what? I'm sick of your crap." Kate retorts, her tone firm. "I'm only hanging out with you because of Bella, but you've crossed the line. Apologize."

Lisa hesitates, her expression shifting from defiance to uncertainty. "Apologize for what? She shoved me, and physical aggression is grounds for expulsion," she counters. Crap. That is why she got into my face, why she pushed my buttons. She wanted me to snap. How could I be so stupid.

I deflate and instantly stop struggling, but before I can sling together a rebuttal, Ben loosens his grasp, steps toward Lisa and interjects, "I'm pretty sure bullying is grounds for expulsion too Lisa. I bet the headmaster would like to know what you said to Amelia."  His tone is calm but firm.

"Like he is going to trust anything that comes out of your mouth, Ben." Lisa spits, "You're already on thin ice as it is. You would know about all the things that can get someone expelled, wouldn't you. Too bad Amelia doesn't have your resources." In a normal situation, I would dissect what she said, but I may be screwed here. There is no way to talk or write my way out of this. I shoved her. God, I'm dumb.

"The headmaster may not believe Ben, but I can enlighten him." Kate says, moving in on Lisa. "In fact, I have lots of things I'm sure he would love to hear about you."

Bella, who has been silent until now, pleads with her sister, "Kate."

"No Bella. She has gone too far for the last time. I'm done sitting back and watching her wreak havoc, and you should be too." The tension between the twins is palpable. Kate turns back to Lisa. "If you report her for pushing you, I'll tell the headmaster what you said to Amelia AND how you threatened Peterson to report his parents to the IRS to get him to drop the journalism class." What in the white-collar crime?

"Seriously, Kate?" Lisa's voice cracks showcasing vulnerability. Who knew she had the depth to feel anything but anger.

"Seriously. Back off your vendetta against the new kids just because you're afraid you'll lose your class ranking," Kate fires back, her tone unwavering. "News flash: Harvard doesn't care what place you're in. You're fourth generation! You're getting in!"

Lisa straightens and is unable to hide the toll of what Kate says to her, even though she tries to play it off. "Whatever, come on Bella." Bella looks between her sister and Lisa conflicted. She lowers her head and follows Lisa out toward the lot.

Kate rolls her eyes and leans back on the lockers, exhaling. "Don't worry, I have enough dirt on Lisa, if she even thinks to go to the headmaster, I can bury her."

"Thanks," I say "but why did you stand up for me?" genuine curiosity replaces my anger.

"I've been sick of Lisa for a while now." she explains "This just gave me the opportunity to cut ties. I just wish my sister could see her for the conniving witch she is, but she can't seem to." Her frustration is evident.

"Well, thanks for choosing now." I reply sincerely.

"You're welcome." She kicks off the lockers set. "See you around."

I nod at her and turn my attention to Ben. "Some bodyguard you are?"

He smirks. "I thought you didn't need a bodyguard."

Is that his move then?

**Benedict**

Damn it, Lisa. I knew she wouldn't listen when I told her to back off Amelia but didn't think she'd act so soon. Normally she is more calculated. I'm surprised by Kate, though. For years she and Bella have followed Lisa around avoiding her warpath. I thought I would have to step in and remind Lisa about the family secrets I know, never guessing her minion to betray her.

Apparently, Amelia didn't need me after all. She was impressive. Standing up for herself and matching Lisa comment for comment. She was justified in pushing her away. Bringing up her mom was a low blow.

Lisa must be desperate, thinking that one push would result in Amelia's expulsion. I broke into the headmaster's office and am still here for crying out loud. Not that I'm proud of it, but Lisa thinking Amelia's mom's past is sufficient to tarnish the reputation of her family is absurd.

The Roberts have been at the school just as long as Lisa's family. They wouldn't expel Amelia out of respect for her grandfather alone. This reinforces my decision to switch schedules. Lisa's next move is uncertain now that she's been publicly embarrassed.

"That's it. I'm transferring to that fancy school just to kick that girl's ass." Sarah Mae sits on the edge of my bed. Her legs crossed with a sketch pad in her lap. I may be short, but Sarah Mae is dainty. We are the same height, however, while I'm curvy, she is thin. Her dark hair is a wisp of curls. I've always loved her hair and questioned how it's always wildly perfect. I admire a lot of things about Sarah Mae. She's small but fiery. While we had originally planned to get together this weekend, I called her on the way home from school to vent. I gave myself two days before telling anyone about the altercation Tuesday.

I knew if I told her she would want to come over immediately and I needed ample time to calm down before facing my mom. I couldn't tell her what Lisa said about her. She'd insist on contacting the headmaster and I don't want to get flagged as a trouble student.

As predicted, Sarah Mae did insist on coming over. Now having her here, I'm not sure how I survived four days without her. I sit across the room in my desk chair laptop open. I've spilled every single detail of my first days at Briarwood, not leaving anything out. Including how Ben has shown up the last two days with an extra coffee for me.

"That would look great on the application" I laugh. "Reason for admission: To kick founding daughter's ass."

"Obviously, I wouldn't put it on the application." She sasses. "You should have punched her in the face."

"I wouldn't even know how to punch someone. I'd probably do it wrong and hurt myself." I try to type out another sentence but stop. "Besides, zero physical aggression policy remember?"

"Ugh fine." Sarah Mae has always been a touch more heated than me. I don't mind standing up for myself, but she is quicker to anger.

"Anyways, I need a break from Days of Briarwood. Tell me about junior year at Wilcocks." I put my laptop down on my desk and lay on the bed next to her.

"It's no different than sophomore year." she sighs "Honestly, I'm a little jealous of you. I bet the art program at Briarwood is amazing and the art teacher isn't also the softball coach." She frowns at her sketch pad. I'm shocked. Sarah Mae isn't the jealous type. With her talent and confidence, I have always looked up to her.

"I thought you loved Coach Stephanie." I say, sitting up enough to lean on my elbows.

72

"I do, I just... ugh! I want more." That is something I understand. It isn't a feeling I'm unfamiliar with. My heart breaks for her.

"Mae Mae" I use her nickname to stress my care for her at this moment. Sitting all the way up, I wrap my arms around her. "With your portfolio, you'll go past getting more. YOU will have it all." I look down at the sketch she has been working on. "Wait, is that me?" She has sketched an image of me in a flowing gown surrounded by thorns. Unlike my nightmare though, I am bursting out of them. "This is incredible."

"Thanks. I wanted you to see how that nightmare you keep having ends." As she speaks I stare at her work, tears threatening to stream out of my eyes. I don't deserve her. "You're going to take that school over."

"Maybe, but only two more years and we are both at college." I smile at her.

"Right," she perks up "but before then I need you to do one thing for me."

"Oh yeah. What's that?" Her requests are never simple and a bit of unease creeps in.

"Give that Ben guy a chance. I think you could use a little fun with all your focus." Nope not happening. She did not.

"I'm sorry did you miss the stalker class schedule change?" I oppose. She cannot be serious.

"Nope. That's my favorite part." She smiles and nudges me with her shoulder "We love protective vibes."

I get up off the bed to move back to my desk "You read too many dark romances."

"And you don't read enough of them." I'm never going to win with her. "Besides, after Tyler it would be good for you to realize not all guys are jackasses."

"I'm not talking about Tyler or seeing any other guys." She knows why I broke up with Tyler. I can't believe she would bring him up. I tried to have a boyfriend once, it didn't work out, I'm done. The only romance I need is on my kindle.

"Look, I get it. He burned you. Bad. But it doesn't mean that you can't try again. Date a little. Dating is like shopping, you don't buy one pair of shoes, you try out several styles, if one pair isn't right for you, you go find another pair."

"Is that why you have 20 pairs of shoes? "I laugh.

"Exactly."

I needed this night. I needed my best friend. In a perfect world, she would have been recruited too. We could take turns driving and I wouldn't have to worry about where I sit at lunch or Lisa cornering me. We would conquer the school together. At least we have tonight.

My mom has never been strict about having Sarah Mae over even if it is a school night, allowing us to spend the rest of the night with her sketching and me working on possible articles and homework. Eventually my mom coaxes us out of my dungeon into the living room for dinner. No more junk food tonight. Gabriel caught wind of our freezer food dinner and prepared meatloaf with my favorite fondant potatoes and glazed honey carrots. There are some perks to living in an inn. I end up falling into bed at 11:30, homework done and belly full. The last thought before I fall asleep is "Dang it. I have to play golf tomorrow."

# Chapter 11

A mistake was made. A colossal, all-encompassing mistake. I'm the ONLY girl taking golf. To make it worse, not only is Ben in the class, he's the teacher's assistant. I've spent the last hour missing every single ball I have tried to hit, then having one of the boys in the class offer to correct my form, to which Ben quickly responds by shooing them away. He has now separated us from the rest of the class and is working with me one-on-one. "Yippee". Can you detect the sarcasm? Thankfully, he hasn't offered to correct my form. Still, he is becoming visibly frustrated with my lack of progress. I'm going to flunk out of private school because I can't hit a damn ball.

"Okay, adjust the placement of your hands. Make sure that your thumb presses down right there." Ben verbally adjusts my feet and my hands for the thousandth time, and I still can't make contact with anything other than grass.

"This is pointless. I'm never going to get it, and I'm probably going to have to add a work-study to pay to replace all the grass I've ruined." My shoulders slump in defeat, feeling just as frustrated as Ben.

"Watch me one more time." It didn't help the first five times, and I doubt it will help now. But I watch as Ben takes his stance. He sets his feet, explains his hand placement, lines up his driver with the ball, and swings back. The ball soars through the air and hits the net at the end of the driving range. He smoothly turns to me, "Your turn." Like it's that easy.

"Ben, I'll never be able to do that." All my confidence is lost. I should've signed up for fencing. At least then I would have a sword.

Ben scrubs his hand over his face and then sighs. "Okay, listen. We can try something new, but I don't know if you will be comfortable with it."

"Ben." I shake my head, knowing exactly what he means, and he is right. I'm not comfortable with it AT ALL. However, the idea of failing wins out. "Ugh, fine."

"I promise, it really is so you can get the feeling of the correct motion, and not feel... anything, um, else." Apparently, he's the one who is uncomfortable. It's actually kind of cute. Dang it, Amelia, no.

"It's fine, desperate times and all of that." I move back to the tee and set my ball up, thankful that I was allowed to trade out my normal uniform skirt with an athletic skort today. Once my ball is set, Ben steps up behind me.

"Ready?" His voice shakes a little as he asks.

"Yeah," but not really. How the hell does he smell this good after being out in the sun all morning? I'm immediately self-conscious about how I smell or that he will be able to feel the sweat on my back. Curse the Georgia heat. Ben steps forward and wraps his arm around me, placing his hands on top of mine. I try to focus only on the way he adjusts my hands, but then he uses his foot to knock one of my feet to widen my stance.

"You have your feet too close together. You have to widen your stance a bit to get more power behind your swing."

"Mm-hm," is all I can manage. Then he glides our arms back, and the feel of his hands on top of mine tingles. He slowly glides our arms back and forth, the movement far smoother than what I managed on my own, but it's hard to focus on anything other than the way he feels pressed against me. I hear him mumble some instructions, but I can't focus on his words. The next thing I know, there is more power to his movements, and our arms come back and swing down. The sound of the driver hitting the ball pops, and I watch as the ball connects with the net. I did it. Kind of.

"Feel the difference." I'm reminded of Ben behind me. He still hasn't released me. A shout from down the range causes him to let go. "What, you can teach her but not us?" One of the boys, whose name I don't know, yells. Then I hear something like "Classic Ben" come from his mouth. The group of boys he's with laugh. The comment grounds me and another red flag waves across my mind.

"Thanks, I got it now." My comment is terse, and Ben scowls in the direction of the boy. I reset the ball and then line my feet up, remembering to take a wider stance and blushing a little at the memory of Ben knocking my feet apart. I take a deep breath, swing back, and to my surprise, I actually hit the ball. It doesn't go as far as when Ben helped me, but I hit it.

Pride swells when I hear Ben shout "That's my girl!" He picks me up and spins me around. I'm so elated and don't even mind. It isn't until he sets me back on the ground that the moment registers, and my cheeks flush again. I back away and smile shyly.

"Thanks," is all I can manage.

I spend the last bit of class hitting the ball almost every time and trying to ignore how giddy I felt in Ben's arms or hearing him call me "his girl." Sarah Mae's words plague my thoughts. There's no denying he is attractive. Objectively, people date in high school all the time, and it never becomes a distraction. Part of the issue with Tyler was that he couldn't imagine life outside of the small town. Ben is already out of that environment. However, there was another big problem with Tyler that I am almost positive would be a problem in any relationship. I doubt this much thought ever goes into buying a pair of shoes.

# Chapter 12

Friday nights are my favorite because in the Roberts home, Friday night is movie night. A tradition long-lived since my childhood. Mom and I stock up on candy, order a cheese pizza, and stream classic movies. Sometimes, we'll watch a trash movie from the 90s, but not tonight. I get to pick tonight, and I chose "How to Steal a Million." Classic Audrey Hepburn. I may have already seen it five or six times, but that isn't the point. When I get home from my afternoon study block, I crash on the couch. My muscles ache. I chose golf because it seemed like the least taxing sport, boy was I wrong. Apparently, swinging a club over and over and over wears on the muscles. I change into some comfortable clothes and fall onto the couch. Mom was nowhere in sight when I got home, which isn't unusual. Sometimes it takes her longer to brief the weekend manager. I start to drift to sleep when the door opening and shutting stirs me.

I listen as Mom shuffles across the room to the couch, but my eyes stay closed. I'm too exhausted to attempt opening them. "Time to wake up, sunshine." Despite her words, Mom's tone tells me she is annoyed. I sense it immediately. Crap. An upset Elizabeth is never good for anyone. On a normal day, she is the epitome of warmth, but when she is annoyed or even worse, angry, the world burns. Opening my eyes, I see her hovering over me.

"What's wrong?" I figure there's no point in delaying it.

She crosses her arms, and the fake sweetness in her voice leaves a knot in my stomach. "Wrong, my little angel, why would you think something is wrong?"

"Because I know you, and you only use pet names when you're about to attack. You lead your prey into a false sense of hope, then pounce." I sit up despite my muscles screaming for me not to.

"Well, my love, is there something you think would be upsetting me?" Not off the top of my head. My blank face spurs her to continue. "Talk to any grandfathers lately?" Crap.

"There may have been a letter," I explain. Her eyebrows raise, "and maybe a phone call or two." Her stare bores into my soul. Lowering my head I admit "We had lunch."

"Amelia, why didn't you tell me?" She's hurt. I can see the look in her eyes. I messed up. I should've told her.

"Mom, I'm sorry. I should have told you. I just didn't want to upset you." She slumps down on the couch next to me.

"Mia," she softens, "I'm not upset you spoke to your grandfather. I'm just upset you felt like you had to hide it." I take her hand and pull her in for a hug. The look on her face kills me.

"I really am sorry. I just know how hard you fought to leave that world, and that Grandpa and Grandma didn't support you. I didn't want you to feel like I betrayed you, but sometimes I wonder what it would be like to have them, you know, as grandparents." She pulls back and smooths my hair down.

"No, I'm sorry. I've been selfish. I didn't want that life and wanted to prove I could make it on my own. I didn't realize I was taking something away from you in the process. I thought I could give you everything you needed here."

Cutting her off, I say, "I do have everything I need."

"No, I know, but you deserve more."

"Mom."

"It's okay, I spoke to your grandfather today." She continues and I sit up straight and stare at her bewildered. To my knowledge, they haven't spoken since Easter.

"You did?"

"He came by. We had our own special lunch," the sarcasm in her voice does not go unnoticed. I search her face for signs of hurt or upset, but she seems relieved. "We talked, and I realized that my pride is a large part of the rift. He wants to start over, and I think that's a good idea." Joy—is that this feeling? No, joy is too simple. What do you

82

describe when after years of secretly hoping for something, it manifests? Relief doesn't quite name it either.

"Really?" I question "There has to be more to it than you guys just talked".

"Yes really, and yes there is more, but none of it paints me in a good light." She sighs. Then she starts to explain. My grandfather had been trying to reach out for years, attempting to repair the rift between my mom and my grandmother. She wouldn't go into too much detail about what caused the rift, but she did say she was guilty of letting anger control her actions. She blamed Grandpa for not standing up to Grandma.

After months of dodging his calls, he showed up to the inn every day this week and refused to leave until she had lunch with him. She only agreed today because he mentioned contacting me. That part of her explanation floods me with guilt. I'm the reason she was blindsided. She assured me that it was okay. The lunch went well. Grandpa finally had a chance to apologize. She admitted to being stubborn about the whole thing. After she finishes, it still feels like a dream.

"And to start this new beginning, we are going to have dinner with your grandparents, at their house. Tomorrow night." Wow, that is soon. I was supposed to sleep over at Sarah Mae's, but I'm sure she'll understand. What should I wear? For holidays, it's always fancy, but then, wait.

"Mom, are you sure about this?" I'm excited, but this can't be easy for her.

She gives me her signature smile, still I notice it is laced with something. "I'm sure. It's time. Now what movie did you choose for tonight?" The subject change is noted. I can ask her more questions in the morning. I give her my own mischievous grin. "How to Steal a Million," she groans, but her heart isn't fully in it. She loves the movie too. "Again? You know it word for word."

I just shrug and she relents. "Fine, but I'm picking the candy."

"Deal."

The rest of the evening is spent pretending that our earlier conversation didn't happen. In our own little world, we laugh and talk through the whole movie, imitating the characters and discussing Simon Dermott's appeal and If he would still be considered handsome today. He would. This is where my happiness truly lies. With Mom in our apartment. Guilt begins to creep up for wanting more, but then it is squashed back down. I think she needs more too.

# Chapter 13

My grandparents' home is a short drive from Briarwood Academy, only about five minutes. When I was little, I'd pretend it was an enchanted castle. The stones and large windows fed my imagination. I'd make myself out to be a lost princess. It helped manage the sense of loss I felt when I'd watch the way my mom and grandparents interacted. So polite. Formal. No warmth. It was a stark comparison to how I would see other grandparents with their grandchildren at school. Every year my elementary school held grandparents' day. The classrooms would be filled with kids and one or even two loving and doting grandparents giving them adoring looks, while I sat alone. I never told my mom.

Once in the third grade, I thought I might work up enough courage to ask but chickened out. It is a day that is burned into memory. I'd snuck off from the annual Easter party.

There were lots of wealthy families there. I wore my favorite blue dress. There weren't many kids, and my mom had gotten sucked into a conversation with my great aunt Sweetie. Yes, that was her real name. Bored and feeling out of place, I hid in my grandfather's study.

He came in and found me curled up in an armchair with a copy of the Briarwood Report. I was reading the editorial page. Glancing up to see him, I knew I'd be in trouble. However, instead of scolding me he asked if I found anything interesting. I told him that I found the editor's report to be biased and lacking support. He laughed a great big laugh, then said, "I think you should tell him; he's by the drink cart." I flustered and hid under the paper. He didn't push, just came, and sat at his desk while I read the paper. Occasionally, he would ask me a question, and I would answer.

At first, his presence was intimidating. After a while, I picked up on a warmth in his voice when he would ask questions or be surprised by my answers. Just as I'd worked up enough courage to invite him to Grandparents' Day, Mom came in and told us it was time to leave. She was on the verge of tears yet held her head high as always. Later I heard her on the phone with Gabriel and learned my grandmother had said something to upset her. That's how every visit ended.

Now standing outside of my grandparent's front door, Mom lacks her normal confidence. She's gone back to the car three times, first for her keys, then her purse, then just to check if it was locked. Like it matters in this neighborhood. Standing side by side this time, I'm in a different blue dress and a white cardigan. Mom wears a black pencil skirt and a blue blouse, the same shade as my dress. We didn't coordinate but do have similar styles. I've been told I'm her miniature several times. I don't have to look over to tell she is nervous; I can sense it. "You know, to get something over with, you have to start" I offer up.

"Right," she nods nervously but then turns back toward the driveway "Maybe I should make sure the car is locked again; I could have hit the unlock button by accident."

"Mom," I level "you're stalling."

"Am I?" she asks, smoothing her hands over her skirt.

"You are. It's going to be okay. We've been here before." Given there were always more people, and with a good amount of effort, my mom could avoid my grandparents altogether if she tried hard enough. "Just ring the bell," I suggest. She takes a breath, nods, and then presses the doorbell. A long chime sounds, and only a moment passes before the door opens, and we are face to face with my grandfather himself. Odd. Anytime we have been here before, a maid opens the door. Yes, my grandparents are paid servants rich. Based on what my mom has said, paid well too.

"Welcome ladies. I wanted to be the first to greet you," my grandfather wears a large smile. "Your mother is just in the sitting room. She's finishing up preparing the drink cart." He motions for us to come in and takes my mom's purse hanging it on a coat rack by the door.

"Hi Grandpa" I add nervously.

"Thanks Dad" Mom says at the same time. The awkwardness could probably be felt at the neighbor's house.

"Well, please follow me. We're glad to have you here," he says as we follow him into a sitting room off the main foyer. The room is decorated expertly. It's the perfect mixture of antique furniture that screams old money but still holds a modern feel. My grandmother stands next to a gold drink cart with glass shelves. She could be on the cover of Home and Garden Magazine. Her hair like she just stepped out of a salon, perfectly styled with what can only be described as country club volume. She's a small woman in heels, probably reaching 5'4. This must be where I get my height from. I don't actually have a lot of memories of my grandmother. She's always too busy at parties playing hostess. This is the first time I've looked at her properly. Clair Roberts.

She turns and smiles, "Welcome ladies. Please come in and make yourselves comfortable." It seems rehearsed, like she's only playing a part. Mom bristles. Grandpa guides us to a small loveseat. He takes a seat in a high-back chair. Grandma glides from the cart and places a martini in my mom's hand. "Still your drink of choice?"

My mom looks surprised but then responds, "Yes, thank you."

"Of course," turning in my direction, she hands me a thin glass full of a reddish-tinted liquid, "A Shirley Temple for Amelia." I take the glass.

"Thank you, Grandma." I try to sound polite, but something feels off.

"Oh, they were your mom's favorite when she was little. That is until she realized there was no alcohol in them. It was worse than when she found out Santa wasn't real," she laughs a little, and my mom blushes. It's a sweet moment.

"Wait, Santa isn't real?" I feign shock. My grandparents both stop laughing and stare at me in horror. It's a joke I would make normally with my mom.

Mom laughs, breaking the tension, "She knows Santa isn't real guys." The relief on my grandparents' faces makes me laugh too. "She's sixteen."

The pair of them recover, and I quickly realize that they probably aren't around many children. Mom is an only child. Grandma sits tall in a matching high-back chair next to my grandfather but doesn't seem to have relaxed as much as him. He is giddy.

"Of course," Grandma's composure returns. "Well, what are 16-year-old girls interested in these days? We don't have much experience."

"Claire," my grandfather warns. The comment is a clear underhanded dig at Mom.

"What, Roland? I'm only trying to get to know our granddaughter." I look to mom for a sign of how to respond but she looks like a lost teenager. I can tell she is regretting this. Coming here, I mean. I feel guilty for wanting this at what it is costing her.

In desperation to end the tension, I say "I'm not sure if I paint the typical portrait of the average teenager." I begin, "School is my main priority, but I enjoy writing. When I'm not writing, I read various novels." I pause thinking of what else to add, "I also like spending time with Mom and my best friend, Sarah Mae." It feels like I'm reading off my CV, but I wasn't sure what she was expecting with her question.

"A focused young woman. I'm impressed," Grandma straightens in her seat. "*Despite your upbringing*", was implied.

"Amelia is an excellent student and brilliant writer," Mom boasts. It seems she has snapped out of feeling chided in hopes of coming to my defense if necessary. She won't allow me to fall under Grandma's scrutiny like her.

Grandpa joins in, "I've read several articles of Amelia's in the Briarwood Report and City News. Such wisdom from a young person is a rarity. Though I'm not surprised. She's been bright since childhood." I feel awkward under his praise. "Your mother was bright too, not that I need to tell you that." He turns to mom, "I'm quite impressed with your business model for your inn, to take such an old establishment and modernize it efficiently while maintaining the charm."

"Thanks Dad" Mom's eyes soften. Out of the corner of my eye, I see my grandmother calculating another comment. Before she can get the chance, I ask, "So grandma, what do you enjoy?" The question catches her off guard. It's almost as if no one has ever asked her. I could have easily asked, "What toothpaste do you use?"

"Well, I run several charity organizations, I'm a member of an antiquing club, and I ," she pauses, collecting herself, "I manage our home." Her last words carry pride. It gives me some needed insight into her character.

"That sounds interesting. What charities do you work with? Mom just helped organize the town rummage sale to raise funds for the children's library." At my words, my grandmother's eyebrows raise. She turns fully to my mom.

"What a noble cause, Elizabeth. Do you often help with charities?" I don't miss how she dodges my question and takes my words as an opportunity to interrogate Mom.

"I help around town when I can." Mom says humbly. I'm not sure why though. She runs most town events and is the first call when anyone needs help raising funds. "I mostly do the event planning for some of the local festivals and events. Proceeds either go to charities or town funds."

"How interesting," Grandma responds, sipping her own drink. I wish she would have picked a different word. A look passes between her and my mom. Something unspoken thickens the air in the room. I like to think I'm the only one who can speak to my mom through our eyes. This is bizarre.

A maid entering the room breaks whatever is transpiring between the two when she announces dinner is ready. The remainder of the evening plays out civilly enough. Grandpa asks lots of questions about school and the paper. Of course, I don't share any Lisa or Ben related details. Mom and Grandma manage to converse without falling into anything resembling a WWE match, so I take that as a win. To an outsider, we look like a normal family. Everyone has baggage, right?

# Chapter 14

The first month of school has flown by. I do well in avoiding Lisa each day. Don't get me wrong; it's not without effort. She has made it clear she is still holding hostility toward me. It only grows each time I have an article selected, especially if hers is bumped. However, she has enough to distract her as tensions between her and Kate have become obvious to everyone in the newsroom. Last week, I overheard some of the kids working on the print machine talking about how they got into it in the parking lot before school. Not that I should care, but Kate is somewhat of a friend. I guess. We work near each other and have "friendly" conversations. She reminds me a lot of Sarah Mae. They would get along well.

Ben still insists on walking me to and from each of my classes. We don't have lunch together though. I've managed to sit in the cafeteria unbothered since the first day, and apparently, he doesn't do the lunch crowd. I don't know where he skips off to every day.

He is probably hiding from Summer. She's remained persistent, watching us as we walk to and from classes. I thought Ben was the stalker. She can't take the hint that he wants nothing to do with her. At first, I felt sorry for her, but not now. Not that it's any of my business or that I care to put too much thought into it. However, he is my friend. I can't deny that after this point. We do spend every day together. He brings me coffee in the mornings. That's what friends do. Right?

I'm in the lunchroom now, looking up at one of the paintings, mulling over these questions. Attempting and failing at avoiding the headache I have from staying up late finishing the Calc homework. I don't care if it isn't due until Monday. I refuse to let math ruin my weekend. I was surprised to find most of my classes no more challenging than at Wilcocks, Calc being the exception. In fact, things are going so well, I have more time than I thought to ponder other things. Ben is an enigma that my brain wants to spend a lot of that time on.

He is handsome, and despite the flirtatious nature that at this point he probably couldn't turn off if he tried, respectful. Never trying to attempt anything more than friendship. We don't talk about dating at all. Books, yes. The paper, yes. The vein in Lisa's forehead that is permanently enlarged, yes. How Summer is lurking as we walk, yes. He always shrugs it off and never gives any inkling he regrets his decision in ending that situationship.

As I continue thinking about the Summer issue, it's as though she is Beetle Juice, but it's thinking of her name three times that summons her to appear in front of me. "Dorothy, right?" Summer's annoyingly high-pitched voice hits my ears as she sits down in front of me. She leans her elbows on the table. "I'm Summer."

Why lunch? Why is it my lunch that keeps getting interrupted? The food here is amazing. Today's shepherd's pie is like Gordon Ramsay himself prepared it. "I know who you are, and it's Amelia." I don't let my annoyance go unnoticed. Ben is the only one who calls me Dorothy. I would like to know how she knows that's his nickname for me. Probably overheard him on one of her stakeout missions.

"Oh good. Ben HAS mentioned me." She perks up and smiles. It is sickly sweet, like an escaped mental patient. "He has mentioned you too."

What is she playing at? Last time I checked, Ben couldn't stand her. Suddenly the reporter in me comes alive. "When would he have time to do that, between avoiding you and trying to get you to take a hint?" Did I say reporter? I meant the witch in me. Normally I'm more collected, but my head hurts, her voice is grating, and I just want my shepard's pie and some peace.

"Oh, you're a funny girl. I didn't realize Ben liked funny girls." She manages to keep her composure even though her smile has become manic. "Listen sweetie, a little word of advice. Ben may be all caught up in this sweet little innocent girl from Kansas act you have going, but eventually he'll get bored." God, what is it with girls at this school trying to give me advice? I can't pretend like her words don't sting, though. Has he been talking about me? Is calling me Dorothy a big joke to him?

"Thanks for the advice, but I think we both know the only thing Ben is tired of is your fake voice, fake nails, and come to think of it, he is just tired of you." I would like to disclose that on a normal occasion, I don't condone bullying or leaning into the urge to get even. Turning the other cheek and all that. However, right now I'm pissed. I'm mad my lunch got interrupted. I'm annoyed it's under the guise of giving advice, when in reality, Summer is peeing on Ben like he is a tree. Finally, I'm enraged by the possibility that my entire friendship with Ben is out of boredom and a chance for him to play with the small-town girl. With that said, civility be damned.

Summer breaks her act. "Listen to me, you little tramp." Oooh, burn. "Ben is mine. He knows it. I know it. Hell, the whole school knows it. He WILL get bored with you and come running back to me like always." Her voice is shrill, her eyes wide, and lipstick slightly fading as she spits while she talks. I thought I only had to dodge spit in Calc.

"Can't wait." I roll my eyes, take a breath, and bite into my shepherd's pie. I refuse to let another lunch be ruined. Summer actually stomps her foot and squeals as she runs off. Wow.

Thursdays are supposed to be my day. I was coming off the high of having another article chosen for the paper. Some of my better work too. A comparison of quoting short form video sounds to the way folklore would travel. It went in-depth into the importance of cultural connections. Now I have to go to Anatomy, angry at Ben, and gosh dang it if it isn't lab today. We have to work together.

I leave lunch a few minutes early to avoid Ben waiting for me in the courtyard. Maybe if I get there quick enough, I can request a different partner today. I have been meaning to expand my social circle. Yeah right. To my dismay, Ben is early too. He's already in the courtyard when I walk through, and any attempt to get by him unnoticed is futile. "Hey Dorothy, ready to spend the next two hours looking in a microscope?" Oblivious, he is.

"Stop calling me that. People are going to start thinking it's my name." I snap and keep walking toward the science building.

"Woah, did I miss something?" He follows after me.

"You did actually. You missed your ex-girlfriend informing me that I'm just an innocent girl from Kansas who has become your plaything." I don't try to hide the fact that I'm hurt or annoyed.

"Wait. What? Amelia. Stop for a second." he begs. I don't though. I keep walking and go through the doors to the science building. "Amelia, come on." Ben moves to catch my hand, stopping me, but I jerk from his grasp. I'm too angry to give in.

"Leave me alone, Benedict." He's silent at my demand but doesn't stop matching my pace until we are in the Anatomy lab, concern on his face. I put my things down and start pulling on my lab coat, prepping the station.

"What do you mean my ex-girlfriend talking to you? Who?" He can't be confused.

"So many exes you lost count?" He's ridiculous, and I can't believe I've wasted this much time thinking of him. I almost considered… You know what, it doesn't matter what I almost considered.

"Please explain. I'm lost here." Dang it, those eyes. Fine.

"Summer, Benedict. You know. Your crazy ex that still follows you around. At least, I thought she was your ex." I really need to calm down. "She came up to me in the cafeteria, told me how you are just playing with me because you're bored."

"Amel- "he tried to interrupt.

"She called me Dorothy." When I say it, the full extent of the hurt hits me. It's silly. It shouldn't matter. If he is just messing with me, we are only friends. It's never gone farther than a few flirtatious comments. Why am I this upset? I look at him properly. He has that look on his face. The one he got when I told him about my first encounter with Lisa. He had it again the first day at golf too, it's a look that says he is about to burn the world down. It doesn't match a boy who is just messing with a girl for fun.

"Only I get to call you Dorothy." He takes my face in his hands, and I suck in a breath at the contact. He leans down and looks me directly in the eyes. "I don't care what Summer said. You. Are. Not. A. Game. Understand?" I would nod but I seem to have lost the ability to speak. He's sincere and demanding. "Words. Amelia." Still nothing, what are words again? He drops his voice. "Say you understand." The lower register of his voice shoots straight through me. The upset and hurt dissipate, and a new feeling blooms.

"I understand." He doesn't let go of my face. We are stuck with his hands on my face as he searches my eyes, as if looking to see if he can believe me. I might actually have forgotten how to breathe.

"Good." He leans closer. "I'm glad you understand that, and one more thing." I have time for a million more things because the entire world has paused "No one else will be calling you Dorothy again. I'll make sure of it." Then he releases me. Just like that. Air fills my lungs, and I'm light-headed. I lean against the lab stool. Right, the Anatomy lab. We are still in school, getting ready for class.

"You don't have to do anything. I handled Summer." Is the only thing I can get out.

He turns to me, leans one hand on the lab table, and uses the other hand to stroke a piece of fallen hair behind my ear. Physical touch is new. It's a line up until two minutes ago he hasn't crossed. I wish I could say I hated it, but I think I might crave it.

"I know you can handle anything Dorothy, but she messed with something that's mine." He says it nonchalantly as his fingers linger near my neck without touching it. The unfamiliar feeling swells in my belly.

"What's that?" I ask so close to his face if I could just lean in a little.

"You are mine." I might faint.

"Your friend, right? You mean I'm your friend." Dumb. Dumb Amelia. You know that isn't what he means.

"Sure, we're friends." Ben pulls back and turns back to the lab table. The rest of the block is incredibly awkward. I miss his hands on my face. The way he tucked my hair behind my ear. I'm completely lost here. I have no idea what to do. I don't think I want to be friends with Ben. The way he called me his felt right. I may want that. I may want that very much.

# Chapter 15

Rain is beautiful. It's the sky opening up and saying, "Golf is cancelled". It's an entire day that I get to spend at home, not reporting to school. I could get a jump start on an article for next week or maybe even hang out with Sarah Mae when she gets out of school before movie night with Mom. I lay in my bed, warm and cozy looking out my window to see the sun shining. The benefit of living in the south and being a good 30 miles from school is that it's raining in Briarwood and the sun is shining here.

I'm feeling well enough that I might even enjoy a cup of coffee on the patio and people watch some of the guests. I can keep myself so preoccupied that I won't have any time to think of Ben or how I'm considering the possibility of expanding our friendship.

A knock at my door springs me into the beginning of not thinking about Ben. "Mia are you up?" Mom's voice sounds through the door.

"Up" I call. "Well awake anyway." The door opens and my mom frantically comes in. She's already dressed for the day in her signature pencil skirt and fitted blouse. Even though the inn has a simple charm, Mom insists on business dress for management. She says it helps elevate to higher-end clientele.

"Okay, so I know that you probably planned on having a relaxing day reaping the benefits of rain in Briarwood, but as it turns out, the inn is also going to get to reap some of those benefits. The country club has some flooding issues due to the rain and now a wedding that was supposed to be held there is being moved here. Even though we normally would never attempt to host a wedding on a day's notice, the father of the bride made me an offer that, quite frankly, I couldn't refuse. Now I need all hands-on deck making this happen." She sounds like she's three cups of coffee into her morning. I don't think she took a breath that whole rant. Exasperated, she collapses at the foot of my bed.

"You want to plan AND set up a wedding in a day? Are you crazy?" I must still be sleeping.

"We don't have to plan this time." She assures me. "They have a wedding planner and all the rentals are booked. As it turns out, we are the only location that has a similar set up. We just need to show around the rental company, decorate, and collaborate with the wedding planner to make sure everything runs smoothly. They even have their own catering." She is trying to convince herself more than me at this point.

I sit up and wipe some sleep from my eyes. "Okay, let me run this back. Everything is planned. Décor and everything else provided. We just have to help facilitate?"

"Yes." mom reassures. Well, if that's all. Ugh! So much for my day off.

"Okay, and did you let Gabriel know that there is an outside catering company coming in? He's fine with it?" I cannot see the in-house chef/my mom's best friend ever being okay with outsider food entering the premises.

"About that... I thought we could tell him together." Mom smiles at me.

"Oh no." I sling my feet out of bed and onto the floor to stride across the room to my wardrobe. "There's no way I'm being a part of that conversation. I will tie tulle and direct vendors all day, but I'm not telling Gabriel that you're letting another chef serve food mere feet from his kitchen."

"Oh, come on. You know he won't yell at you." She's senile.

"I will come in after and do damage control. Final offer." I start pulling out a pair of comfortable black slacks and a sleeveless white dress shirt. If I have to work today, I'll need to dress professionally as well. Vendors won't like taking directions from a teenager, especially if I go in with the sweatpants I had planned for today. I will mourn you faded gray sweats. Another day.

"I'll take it." Mom beams and comes over to hug me from behind. "Thank you. I owe you. I know this isn't how you wanted to spend your day."

I place my hands on her arms and lean into her embrace. "Don't thank me yet, thank me with Chinese takeout and a makeup movie night if we get through this."

"How about I throw in a new pair of shoes too?" I choke a little and then laugh it off, thinking of Sarah Mae's earlier metaphor.

"I'll be down in a bit." With all my clothes in hand, I move to the bathroom to start getting ready. Having my own bathroom is one of the perks of living in a renovated inn.

By the time I make it downstairs, all chaos has unleashed. The inn's been invaded inside and out. There are countless vendors dressed in white button-ups and ties. I blend right in. In the crowd, I catch a glimpse of my mom by the reception desk in a lively conversation with a woman in a bright pink suit and matching 6-inch stilettos. She looks like she went shopping in Dolly Parton's closet. Her hair is even styled like the iconic singer. My money is on either wedding planner or the mother of the bride.

I approach the two and Mom spots me. "Oh good, Celia, this is my daughter Amelia, I was telling you about."

The most southern accent I have ever heard comes from this woman's mouth, which is a feat considering we live in Georgia. "Amelia, it's a pleasure. I'm just so gosh darn happy that we were able to secure a venue this soon." I take her perfectly hot pink manicured hand. "I cannot wait to work with you today. Your mom tells me that you will run point for vendor set up?"

"Yes ma'am. I can do that and anything else you need today." My own accent comes out thicker than intended. Mom bumps my arm. I stand taller and try to imitate some of the confidence she has. If this is as big of a payday as she says, it has to go well.

"Well, butter my biscuits. This is just great. You know when Clair mentioned your little inn as a replacement option, I wasn't convinced. I mean, I had heard y'all had done some smaller scale weddings, but something of this scale."

Mom interjects, "I'm sorry, Clair?"

"Yes, Clair Roberts. She is friends with the bride's mother. She was at the club when we realized the flooding had ruined our ceremony location, and of course, an indoor wedding was out of the question."

"I'm going to have to apologize. I need to hear that again." Shocked by the news of grandma's suggesting our inn. Mom asked for clarification "My mother. Clair Roberts?"

Celia, not taking this as anything out of the norm. "Yes, yes, of course, dear. She went on and on about how beautiful your grounds were and insisted I come check this location. As always, she was right. Stunning grounds and charming interior. This may just be one of the best weddings I have ever thrown."

Mom, still in a state of shock, loses her composure so I jump in. "Well, we are glad to host you. Where would you like me to get started?"

Celia goes into a list of things that need to get done causing Mom to jump back into full *Lizzie Mode*, moving around and directing people. With the newly bestowed wedding clipboard in hand, I begin guiding vendors around the inn. First, the tables and chairs are set up off the back porch for the reception. They will still have a view of the pond but be far enough away so no ducks should try to hit the dance floor. Next, chairs for the ceremony and setting the arbor up near the 100-year-old magnolia tree. I've seen many weddings under this tree. When we were little, Sarah Mae and I would have tea parties out here and have our Barbies get married using lantana flowers as bouquets. After the ceremony sight is well underway, I direct florists and decorators. It isn't until the caterers show up to start prepping for the rehearsal dinner that I take a break.

Now is as good a time as any to go into the kitchen to see how Gabriel is taking the news. "Salmon puffs, they are serving salmon puffs! It's a disgrace!" I hear him before entering the swinging doors. As I come in, "Amelia, good, one sane person. Did you know they are serving salmon puffs?" Gabriel is fuming in his black chef's coat and matching bandana. His normally tan skin, now showing shades of red. He is tall and gorgeous and would be any woman's dream. His husband Michael crushes those dreams.

"How did you manage to get the menus this fast?" I laugh. Going straight to the prep station I steal a piece of carrot and pop it into my mouth.

"I have my ways" he responds. "You should be thanking me. This menu is uninspired. When does the wedding party get here? I've prepared my own dish to help them see they have better options." I don't doubt it.

"Gabriel." I say firmly "You cannot order and prep an entire wedding worth of food in a night. We don't have the staff. However, I'll be working the event and will surely perish with only salmon puffs as an option." I smile. "Sooooo, if you wanted to make me my own special Amelia wedding relief dish, you would save me from becoming malnourished."

"This girl." He throws his hands up. "I will concede only if you promise to offer some of my appetizers during the rehearsal dinner. This menu says nothing about platters for the rehearsal dinner. They need something as the wedding party and family arrives."

"You and I both know if I serve your appetizers tonight, they will insist on switching caterers. We don't have the time." The ego stroke is just what he needs to relent.

"Fine." He pouts.

"You know, the wedding party did book rooms for tonight." I raise my brows. "Which means breakfast in the morning is all you? Think of all the different options you could prepare. The fruit plate sculptures you could do for the bridal suite."

"My beautiful girl, I love the way you think." Gabriel smiles. He is calm and now I get the appetizers he has prepared for lunch. A win-win if there ever was one.

As I exit the kitchen ready to return to vendor directing duties, I run smack dab into a very hard chest. I stumble a little attempting to gain my bearings, ready to apologize profusely to... Ben? Standing in a dark blue dress shirt, khaki pants, with his hair perfectly styled is Ben, who is looking at me slightly taken aback.

"Doro- I mean, Amelia." He adjusts. He is standing with two men, one that looks similar to him but a few years older and a much older man who could be in his 50s to 60s. It's hard to tell.

"Hi Ben. What are you doing here?" I don't address the men with him, but they look at me with interest.

"My brother is getting married." He takes in my appearance. "Do you work here?"

"Kind of. This is my mom's inn." I gesture around me.

The older man interrupts. "Benedict, are you going to introduce us to your... friend?"

Flustered. "Sorry Dad. This is Amelia Roberts. We go to school together."

"Roberts?" He takes it in. In his deep voice. "Roland's granddaughter? Well, I'll be. Nice to meet you young lady. Your grandfather is a friend of mine, good man."

"Thank you sir. It's nice to meet you. Mr. Blake, I presume." I stick my hand out very professionally. He takes it and shakes firmly.

"I'm Brody, also the groom." The younger guy interjects smiling. "Nice to meet you, Amelia. Beautiful place you and your mom have here."

"Thank you and congratulations on the wedding." I'm still surprised to see Ben here, but I try to remain professional. "Well, let me know if y'all need anything, but I should get back to set up. We want the rehearsal dinner to run smoothly." I nod politely.

Brody responds, "Of course, we don't want to keep you."

I take the opportunity to rush back outside. As I reach the door, I look over my shoulder. Sure enough, Ben is staring. There goes no thinking of him today.

# Chapter 16

No one in the history of the world has ever been as tired as I am. Okay, maybe one or two people, but exhaustion doesn't even begin to describe how I feel. I'm running on coffee, the promise of snagging the appetizers Gabriel prepared to steal the show, and pure will. In a matter of ten hours, the inn has been transformed. Magnolia Manor has become a wonderland of twinkling lights and white tulle with light blue and gold accents. It feels like I've stepped into a fairy tale wedding. Hats off to Celia.

I'd worried at first when all the tulle arrived that we would be faced with a gaudy affair but was surprised by the simple elegance of everything. Just off the back porch, a platform dance floor has been built with tables spanning around it. The head table is beautifully decorated with various shades of hydrangeas. It's now nearing 6:15, with a rehearsal start time of 6:30. I've changed into a slender black dress to help oversee the proceedings while still blending in with the serving staff. Mom and Celia talk animatedly near the caterers' tent, no doubt congratulating each other on a job well done.

The sun is beginning to set, and the view of the light reflecting off the pond is stunning. Tired or not, I take a moment to appreciate the magic of it all.

"Beautiful," I'm startled from my momentary trance by Ben's voice. I turn to see him in sleek navy dress pants paired with a light blue button-down, sleeves rolled up. His brown hair is perfectly styled. His shirt, combined with all the blue accents around us, makes his eyes pop. I'm almost too stunned to speak. Almost.

"It really is. Your soon-to-be sister-in-law has excellent taste," I smile and move to try and remind myself that I'm still working.

"I wasn't talking about the decorations," Ben responds, making my cheeks flare. I duck my head, trying to think of what I should be doing right now.

"Anyway, the wedding party can go stand by the drink cart to wait for the bride and groom to come down." I head over to a small side table that holds a laptop and speaker. I turn on the music selected to play while the guests of the rehearsal dinner arrive. Suddenly instrumental music fills the air loudly, and it startles me. I jump and immediately lower the volume. Ben chuckles as he approaches me from behind. When I turn around, he's standing far too close. The sound of the piano and violin mixed with how good he smells and looks, causes my senses to go into overdrive.

"Let me get all my facts together. Your mom owns the inn, and you work here in your free time?" he inquires. Ben should really be waiting with the other party guests.

"Yes." It is a simple answer, but words aren't really coming right now.

"Yes? That's all, Dorothy? Usually, you're chattier, especially when you are arguing that Emily Dickinson was ahead of her time." He is trying to goad me.

"A. She was. And B. It was a yes or no question. If you were expecting more, you should have been more specific," immediate regret. I should know by now Ben is always looking for an opening.

"My apologies. What else do you do in your free time?" he corrects.

I try to avoid thinking about you. No, not what I should say. "I don't know. I hang out with my mom and my friend Sarah Mae. Why the sudden interest in my personal life?" Ben being here today was a surprise, but I've managed not to run into him again since this morning. Which would indicate he has no interest in me outside of the school environment. Not that I have had too much time to consider that with all the work I've been doing today.

"I'm curious. You don't talk about it, and now I have a chance for an inside scoop. Who is Amelia Roberts? Published author, investigative reporter, okay golfer, and part-time innkeeper?" He gives me one of his award-winning smiles, and I'm transported into the same world I'm always in with him. Over the last month, this has happened a lot. We talk and laugh, and I forget momentarily that anything exists outside of the two of us.

"I guess a full-time innkeeper. My mom and I also live here. We have our own private apartments on the top floor away from the guests' rooms. I help sometimes after school or with special events." Ben follows me around as I check off a few things on my clipboard.

"Wait. You live here? You have access to this view every day?" He sounds truly jealous. "That is pretty cool." There is no teasing.

"Yeah. I guess it is." I smile up at him.

"So. Does that means you will be at the wedding tomorrow?" I see an idea brewing behind his eyes.

"Yes. Why?" I question. His eyes light up. Something is definitely brewing.

"Will you be working the event, or would you be allowed to participate?" he asks. Participate?

"I mean, I don't think the bride would appreciate me trying to marry your brother, if that's what you are asking," I chuckle.

"No, I just meant that if at the reception, if you were asked to dance by a guest. Would that be allowed?" He looks nervous.

"I have danced at weddings before, yes." Is Ben asking me to dance with him?

"You get asked to dance at weddings? By whom?" There is Ben from golf. The one who looks like he might get into a fight.

"Usually, men old enough to be my grandfather and the occasional ring bearer," this conversation is ridiculous. A memory of me and Tyler at a wedding last summer comes to mind. He offered to help with preparations as an excuse to come over, and during the wedding, we slipped off near the pond to dance. That was my first kiss. I don't think I should tell Ben that, though.

His face relaxes, and just as he's about to respond, we are interrupted by none other than Lizzie Roberts herself. "Amelia, who is your friend here?" Real subtle, Mom. I take a step back, remembering where we are. At this point, most of the wedding party has arrived, and I'm holding Ben up.

"Mom, this is Benedict Blake, brother to the groom. We go to school together." As I speak, she appraises him, then realization hits her.

"Your mentor, Ben?" She has absolutely no tact and still has not addressed Ben directly. He doesn't seem to mind and instead sees an opportunity.

"Amelia has mentioned me?" Not what he should be focused on. "She's told me wonderful things about you, Ms. Roberts. It's nice to meet you." He's all charm, but I wish he knew it was wasted. Lizzie Roberts will chew him up and spit him out.

"You can call me Lizzie," mom says sweetly. What in the world? "It's nice to meet a school friend of Amelia's. As much as I would love to chat more, I'm sorry. I need to steal her away." She slips her arm into mine. "We have a few things to tend to. Enjoy the rehearsal dinner." She nods and pulls me away. Ben runs his hand through his hair. I watch as Mom pulls me toward the kitchen entrance as he walks toward the wedding party.

"Jesus Mom, that was smooth," I say as we stumble into the kitchen.

"Don't *Jesus Mom* me," she looks like a cat about to pounce. "THAT is your mentor?"

"Yeah, and..." the kitchen is quiet. Dinner service was shut down tonight to eliminate the traffic through the inn. Apparently, an additional large payment was made to compensate us for our losses. It must have been very large because even Gabriel took the night off happily.

"The way you described him, he might as well have been a troll under a bridge. You didn't tell me he looked like that." She pinches my arm. "You've been holding out on me?"

"Ouch!" I rub my arm. "Holding out on you?"

"Amelia, that boy is gorgeous. Do you not have eyes?" I didn't expect this reaction from her. I thought she was angry that I was talking to a boy.

"I mean, yeah. He's cute. I guess." I don't want to tell her, *I know! Every day is a constant struggle.*

"You guess. Why didn't you tell me? You barely want to talk about school other than classes. Is there something I should know?" Dang it, she's hurt.

"No. I mean... I guess I kind of like him, but it doesn't matter. Remember, after Tyler, I swore off boys."

"Oh, sweetie," she pulls me in for a hug. "I know that the Tyler situation was tough. Don't get me wrong, I have thought of many ways to hurt him without getting caught. However, that doesn't mean you have to swear off ALL boys."

I pull back. "I just thought, you know, after everything, you wouldn't want me dating."

"Let me be clear. I don't want you to date Tyler. He's immature and not good enough for you." Her voice is level and stern. "But dating, liking boys, it's normal for a girl your age. I want you to have a normal childhood."

I contemplate her words. I've been entirely dead set on avoiding relationships and dating completely. I just assumed she felt the same. "I didn't know you felt that way."

"The only reason I didn't bring it up is that I didn't know you were interested in anyone, or that your mentor looks like that."

"He is really handsome," I smile. I feel like a weight has been lifted. I've been wanting to talk to her about this for a month.

"Yes, handsome would describe the rom-com star," she deadpans, but I can see a smile forming.

"That's what I thought of him at first too!" We really are cut from the same cloth.

"Well, now that we have cleared this up, I think you should be off duty for the rest of the night. I'm not saying you have to go to bed, but maybe eat, relax, enjoy a good book in the sunroom." The sunroom that has a perfect view of the backyard.

"Thanks Mom. I am exhausted."

"Me too. After the rehearsal, I'll have the weekend manager finish clean up and I'll come up. Thank you for all your help. I don't think I could have pulled this off without you." She wraps me in another hug.

"All part of the star daughter package," I shrug.

"I really did get lucky with you. Just remember, the star daughter can have some fun too. PG fun, to be clear, but some fun." I love my mom.

## Benedict

What are the chances that my brother's wedding gets moved to Amelia's inn? I was shocked to see her earlier today. I was bummed golf got canceled. Then I spent the entire morning helping Brody calm an inconsolable Alyssa down. He called me this morning, panicked from the country club when they realized the patio would never dry in time for setup.

Alyssa has dreamed of an outdoor wedding since she was a little girl. She deserves it too. Unlike most debutantes in the circles we run, Alyssa is as far from snobby as it gets. She has a heart of gold. I'm still questioning why she's with my brother. My mom loves her. Alyssa sits with her through her chemo sessions. She has really helped out this past year.

Clair Roberts saved the day when she recommended Magnolia Manor as a replacement venue. I should have made the connections sooner but was under the impression Amelia wasn't close to her grandparents. There are rumors, but her mom seems to be doing well here. This place is beautiful, and I'm jealous of the view of the pond from the back porch. An image of Amelia sitting on one of the rockers with a book in hand or her laptop balanced on her lap comes to mind.

The last month has been torture. I flirt with her constantly, but she never takes the hint. I've tried to take things slow and get to know her. I get the feeling she has probably been burned in the past, the way she talks about fictional men being the only honorable ones in discussions. I was livid when I found out Summer confronted her. She really is clueless. I set the record straight later that day, and of course, Summer pouted and begged me to go into an empty classroom for old times' sake. A make-out session isn't what I want. I would take one conversation with Amelia over kissing Summer any day.

I know it has been a lot of stress for everyone moving the wedding last minute but thank God for rain. I finally get a chance to see Amelia outside of school. She is more relaxed and carefree. I've been able to catch glimpses of her throughout the day. She directed vendors this way and that way, smiling and laughing, in control. She had grown men taking directions from her. It was hot. Then when I saw her looking out at how all her hard work had paid off, I was awestruck. There is no way I'm leaving this weekend without telling her how I feel. Even if it's just for a moment, one dance on the dance floor. This is the chance I have been waiting for.

The light from my window filters in through the sheer curtains. I slept harder than I have in months. Nothing like putting together an entire wedding in less than 24 hours to ensure a good night's sleep. It's strange, waking up and realizing that technically Ben slept under the same roof.

After devouring my dinner in the kitchen, I watched a bit of the rehearsal dinner from the sunroom. Brody and his bride-to-be really do look like they are in love. Ben is different with his family. At school, he's always confident and flirty. Watching him interact with his brother, he's more serious. Like he has a weight on his shoulders. I want to ask him about it.

My talk with Mom resonated with me. I guess because of her past and my own bad experiences, I assumed she would be hostile toward any boy that looked at me. I couldn't have been more wrong. She trusts me, and really does want the best for me. With that new knowledge, I'm nervous about today. I had been considering the possibility of Ben. However, here in my safe haven the great expectations of Briarwood disappear, and we are left with just Amelia and Ben. Well, Amelia, Ben, and a wedding to put on. With that final thought, I lunge myself out of bed and get ready for the day.

The smell of coffee lures me from my room, and I find Mom at the island still dressed in her pajamas. "Late start?" I ask.

"It's only 7, and the weekend staff is prepped for today's event. You did such a great job yesterday there isn't much to do today other than enjoy." She pauses, taking a large sip of her coffee. "We have time for coffee and breakfast."

I float over to meet her. The smell of the coffee overtaking me. "Coffee first. I like it."

"I thought you might." Mom is polite enough for me to take a few sips before she begins. "Tell me more about Ben."

I choke on my coffee. "I told you about him last night."

"No, you told me that and I quote, 'you guess you like him.' I need more details." She moves back toward the toaster oven and takes out some frozen waffles.

"I mean…. I don't know. What do you want to know?" It's too early and I don't have enough coffee in my system for this.

"Mia, you've been holding out on me for over a month now. I want to know everything I missed." We don't have nearly enough time for everything.

I go into explaining how Ben started out a little flirty and how we have some classes together. I talk about how frustrating he can be in literary discussions, always challenging me. How he brings coffee to Journalism and how his sports articles actually make the events he covers interesting. How his calculus notes mysteriously appeared in my locker after I had a meltdown the day before my first test. I go into some detail about Lisa and Summer. I leave it with him kind of asking me to dance tonight.

"Let me clarify. You have become the female lead in your own personal romcom, and you have given me nothing!" She exclaims.

"It's not like that. He's just my mentor and kind of flirty friend." I put my head into my arms.

"Amelia. A boy does not bring you coffee every day or basically growl at other boys when he doesn't like you."

"Oh my God Mom! He doesn't growl at them, he just scowls." Realization hits me. I did see him after golf one day towering over a guy who was trying to chat with me walking through the course.

"Same thing. Amelia, I'm happy for you. Don't get me wrong, I love how driven you are by school and how focused you are, but I want to see you living a little too. I've been worried about you, socially." I had no idea.

"I'm not a hermit." I grumble. "I have friends. Well, I have Sarah Mae and you."

"I know that. As much as I hate to admit it, you need more than just us. You need friends at school too." She takes a breath. "A very cute boyfriend isn't what I had in my mind, but I will take it as a start."

"Mom! Ugh! He isn't my boyfriend." She laughs at my response.

"Well, maybe not yet, but you two are heading in that direction."

"Can this conversation end, please?" I start cleaning up my breakfast dishes.

"For now, because we really do need to be downstairs. But honey, it really isn't a bad thing." She moves to her room. "He seems like a nice boy."

I respond with an eye roll. I head downstairs to start the very hectic day of avoiding my mom and making sure this wedding runs smoothly.

I'm on bridal suite duty today. So far, it has been simple. Gabriel came through with making sure the bridal party had any snack or drink they could ever want stocked and ready to go. He even made a watermelon replica of the gazebo with a tiny fruit bride and groom.

The bride, Alyssa, is stunning. She is as far from a bridezilla as one can be. She's constantly checking in on everyone else, making sure they are happy. Her bridesmaids have reminded her several times it is her day. She keeps asking about Brody's mom, if she has arrived. I might have done some eavesdropping and learned that Ben and Brody's mom has been battling cancer. No one was sure she would feel up to the wedding today. It explains why Ben is different with his family. They've gone through so much this past year. I feel bad for not knowing. He never lets on about anything at school.

"Okay ladies, is there anything else I can get for you?" I ask before ducking out to check on the time. The ceremony will be starting soon.

"No. Thank you, Mia. You've been wonderful." Alyssa calls. I told Alyssa to call me Mia. She is too kind not to allow her the invitation.

"Okay" I chime. "I'll come back when it's time to go down." As I slip out of the room, I hear the girls gushing over her, telling her how excited they are for her again.

Coming down the hall to the lobby, I spot Ben with an older woman in a wheelchair. He is knelt next to the chair, looking up at her with a soft expression. This must be his mom. She is frail although you could tell at one time she was the picture of beauty. I'm too far away to hear them, but Ben looks up at me, and my heart stops. He gives me a breathtaking smile as he stands. He's wearing a full black tux. I may swoon.

"Amelia, I want to introduce you to someone." He waves me over.

I approach the pair, and the woman appraises me. "Mom, this is Amelia Roberts. Amelia, this is my mom, Grace." Ben's voice is tender as he speaks.

"Hello, ma'am, it is nice to meet you." I straighten my posture and smile politely, feeling a strong need for her approval.

"Ma'am, you do not have to call me ma'am dear.  You can call me Grace." She huffs.

"I'm sorry. It is nice to meet you, Grace." I correct myself.

"It's nice to meet you finally Amelia. Ben has told me a lot about you," I seem to have already earned her approval. I'm surprised.

"He has?" I raise an eyebrow at Ben.

"I've mentioned you once or twice," Ben rubs the back of his neck, clearly rethinking his choice of introducing me to his mom.

"I see," I smile at him, then turn my attention back to his mom. "I hope all good things. If it's okay with you, I'd like to let Alyssa know you're here. She's been asking about you."

"Oh, that girl. She's always making such a fuss over me. Someone ought to remind her this is her day." I like Grace already.

"Oh, her bridesmaids have reminded her." I reassure her.

Ben stares at me and his mom conversing like this isn't our first meeting. After spending all my time this morning in the Bridal Suite, I feel like I'm a part of the family. Not that I want to be. I just... Shut up, Amelia.

"Okay, Mom, let's get you to your seat. We have a spot for you in the shade." Ben goes to wheel his mom away but then steps back. "I'll see you later, Dorothy? On the dance floor?" My heart flutters a little.

"Yeah," I nod. "I'll be around."

**This day is unreal. I scurry off back to the bridal suite.**

# Chapter 18

That was the most beautiful and heartfelt wedding I have ever been to, and I have been to a lot of weddings. Alyssa and Brody may as well be a prince and princess. They even wrote their vows. I cried twice. Now I'm standing off near the catering tent listening to Celia rant about how she has never worked with a better couple. I believe her. She's also been regaling the staff with wedding horror stories. She's traded in her bright pink attire for a softer light pink which she says is because she would never attempt to steal the spotlight from a bride.

I'm pretending it's her antics that have kept me locked into place here and not the nerves of Ben possibly asking me to dance at any moment. Not that he would have a chance. Alyssa's niece and flower girl Jules has kept him busy. The fiery little four-year-old pulled him onto the dance floor the first chance she got. Anytime he attempts to break away she puffs her lip out. It's sweet how he humors her. Not that

I've been staring at them. It's hard not to notice. They are adorable.

I spot Brody coming over to the pair of them and bowing to Jules as he extends his hand. Ben has a momentary look of relief before mouthing thanks to Brody. Alyssa is at the head table smiling at the scene. She likely orchestrated the interruption. Ben starts to scan the room and I try to duck behind a pillar so I'm not caught spying. When his eyes meet mine, I know I'm out of luck. As he moves toward me, I startle and almost take a waiter out. Fortunately, he dodged out of my way. I mumble an apology. He assures me it happens all the time. By the time I recover, Ben is fully in front of me.

"Avoiding me again Dorothy?" he asks smirking. I knew on day one that smirk would be the end of me.

"I'm not avoiding you" I straighten. "You seem to be quite entertained without me." I say falling into our normal flirtatious behavior. "Jules is quite the dance partner."

He laughs it off "Watching me, Amelia? I thought I was your stalker."

I gasp. "I —" don't have a response.

"It's okay. Jules is adorable. But I don't think she'll mind too much if I switch partners for a bit." He is incredulous.

"Well, you have your pick." I wave my hand as if to offer him the whole floor.

He buttons up his jacket that he loosened earlier and stands tall. "So it would seem" he says looking over the dance floor. Playful Ben has arrived. He stands in front of me and bows. "Amelia Roberts, I am no older gentleman or ringbearer, but may I have this dance?" He looks at me through hair that has fallen in his eyes. I want to take his hand but messing with him is too much fun.

"I don't know. I don't usually settle for groomsmen." He holds his hand to his chest as if I have wounded him. I giggle then say, "I guess I can make an exception."

"Yes." He breaks character and balls his hand into a fist. He's incredibly goofy. Taking my hand, he leads me to the dance floor as a violin starts to play. I recognize the tune but there are no lyrics. I think it's a Taylor Swift song. Ben wraps one hand around my waist and takes my hand in his as I place my other on his shoulder. It's formal, but I'm relaxed in his arms. He leads us into a Walz. Ben can Waltz?!

After an uncomfortable silence, I take a chance and look up. My first mistake of the night, because the way Ben looks at me ensures that I fall. I break every single rule I have ever made. I'm willing to throw out every hesitation I've ever had. I let myself not only want him in that moment but have him. We don't speak. We just looked at each other. He spins me around and around and something clicks. By the time the song ends we stand still. He doesn't release me. Then another song begins, and I go to move away but Ben pulls me back a little closer.

"One more?" he whispers. It's a request and a plea.

"Okay." I reply softly.

We dance for three more songs.

126

"I have to admit something to you" Ben says finally. "I've wanted to ask you out for a while."

"Oh," I breathe into him. My god he smells good. "And why haven't you?"

"Honestly? I didn't want to push. You made it clear that you didn't want to go out, but then you flirt. I guess I was just waiting."

"I mean, I didn't want to." I try to muster up some sort of courage.

"Didn't but now you might?" He sounds hopeful.

"I could maybe be open to the possibility of going on a date. If I was asked." I can't make it too easy for him.

"Say I was to ask. What would Amelia Dorothy Roberts want to do on a date?" he spins me out and around.

"First, my middle name is Jane, and second, I might want to go to the fall festival in town next weekend." I answer with my own smirk.

"Two weekends in Amelia's world?" he grins fully. "In that case. Amelia, will you go to this fall festival with me next weekend?"

"I mean I would have to check and make sure I'm free" I draw out. He pulls me closer. "Yes, I would."

"Yes!" He exclaims. We fall into a steady rhythm with the music before he breaks the happy silence, "I have to ask though. Why now? Was it dancing with Jules?"

"Actually, I had a talk with my mom." How much do I tell him?

"Your mom told you to go on a date with me?" He sounds genuinely intrigued.

"No. Well yeah. No, I just." I stop and take a breath. "So, before school started, I had a boyfriend. It ended badly so I swore off boys. Then I met you and I liked you, but I wasn't sure I wanted to date again. Then my mom and I talked, and she let me know that not all boys suck." I'm rambling.

"Remind me to thank your mom," he says wholeheartedly. Then is quiet for a moment considering his next words. "This other boyfriend, what do you mean in ended badly?"

I don't want to have this conversation with him. "He just didn't respect some boundaries. He also hated the idea of me going to Briarwood. He kind of flipped when I got my acceptance letter."

"He sounds like an idiot." It's a fair conclusion.

"He is," I laugh it off.

"Well, I should thank him too." Ben pulls me flush.

"Why?" I ask relaxing into him.

Ben whispers into my hair "Because now I get to go on a date with you." Then he lightly kisses the top of my head.

My second mistake of the evening. I have fallen for Ben, and we haven't even gone on a date yet.

**Benedict**

This is the best day ever, and not just because I can finally stop hearing about how Brody can't wait to marry the love of his life. Today is the best day ever because today is the day I asked Amelia on a date, and she said yes. I have a date with Amelia. I got to dance with Amelia. She was beyond beautiful in her light blue dress. It looked like it was custom-made for her.

Everywhere she moved today, she caught someone's attention. I was jealous at first, but it's like she comes alive here. There's no hesitation in her actions. She is unmovably sure of herself. When I first caught her watching me and Jules dance, I was ecstatic. I half expected her to hide away all night. I tried to break away, but I have a soft spot for Jules. Alyssa brings her around, and she is the cutest little girl. No one can tell her no. I'll have to buy her a big teddy bear for helping me impress Amelia.

When she agreed to dance with me, I felt like I won a month-long marathon. Then when she agreed to go out with me. Man. I didn't want to pry, but I do want to know more about her ex. Any guy who is stupid enough to lose her had to have messed up royally. She tensed up talking about him. What did she mean, didn't respect her boundaries? Does she still see him around? Suddenly I'm jealous of a guy I've never met.

I need to take a breath. All that matters right now is I have a date to plan. I looked for her after the send-off, trying to get a few extra minutes, but I couldn't find her. She must have been busy helping with clean up. I'll have to ask around in the morning about this fall festival.

# Chapter 19

I feel like I'm floating. I have a date with Ben. A real date. This weekend has been surreal. Not only having Ben in my world but getting to see a glimpse of his. We only separate once it is time to do the send-off. I had to remind myself that I was still working. I left Ben with the hope of seeing him again before the night was over, but that plan was quickly squashed at the sight of my mom with my grandparents. I didn't see them come in. It makes sense that they are here though; Grandma did suggest the venue, she must be friends with the Blakes.

I see the three of them standing toward the end of the back porch in a deep conversation. A quick study shows nothing seems to be too off. Mom isn't holding her normal defensive stance when talking to my grandmother. I still approach with caution.

"Grandma, Grandpa, what a surprise!" I address them warmly. Grandpa attempts to wrap me in a hug, but it's a bit awkward.

"Amelia dear, we were just congratulating your mother on a successful event," he says.

"Yes, we didn't want to intrude earlier as you both looked busy," Grandma adds. I'm still getting used to her. She seems like she wants to be civil but isn't sure how to without coming off condescending.

I move to Mom, wrapping my arms around her waist. "Oh, Mom is the best at pulling off the impossible."

Mom puts her arm around me. "I couldn't do it without my partner. Amelia was such a huge help yesterday and today."

"Yesterday? Amelia, did you miss school to help with the event?" My grandma asks with concern in her voice. I wouldn't be surprised if she tried to call child services.

"No. Friday is specials day and I have golf. It was canceled because of the rain." I rush to mom and my own defense.

"Oh, I see." She rolls her shoulders back and smooths her skirt. "You play golf?"

I laugh off her question. "Not well. I just picked it because I had to have a P.E credit. I'm not very good."

"I play golf." My grandfather interjects a little unsure. "I could help you if you wanted."

I beam up at him. "I would like that."

My mom stiffens, and a look to her "I'm sure we can work something out. Mom, Dad, it was great to see you, but we need to get started on cleanup. Mom, thank you again for

132

the recommendation. Dad, I'll call about lunch." Lunch? What did I miss?

After saying goodbye to my grandparents, Mom and I don't go straight to cleanup. Mom pulls me upstairs. She looks a bit panicked. By the time we reach our apartment, I half expect her to explode.

"She takes credit for something I did! I did! Okay yes, she mentioned that we have an inn here and the grounds are beautiful, and we have built a rather good reputation, right?" I don't respond. "Right. But here is the thing. I built that. Me. I didn't have her help. Then she makes one little comment and now that we have pulled off the wedding of the century, she talks about how I will have all this business coming my way and I will be on the map. On the map! Well, let me tell you something lady, I was already on the map! It just wasn't her map!" She finally takes a breath.

"I'm assuming we're talking about Grandma." I stare at my mom with full sympathy.

"Yes we are talking about Grandma. Who else?" She moves and collapses on the couch, pulling a throw pillow out from under her and squeezing it. I sit on the arm of the couch at her feet.

"I feel like I'm missing some information here." I say looking down at her. "Want to fill me in?" This is one of those moments where for a while we aren't mother and daughter. We are best friends and right now my best friend is hurting.

Mom goes into a recount of her conversation with Grandma and Grandpa. Apparently, spy needs to be added to my grandmother's list of jobs because that is what she was doing the entire ceremony. Spying on Mom and me.

She waited until Mom was completely done and received a big fat check from Celia before she swooped in. Grandma started out by congratulating Mom on pulling off such a glorious event. She made snide comments about how she always knew Mom would like this life. Event planning, as if that is all she does. She basically implied that the life she ran from now surrounds her.

Then she started on all the business Mom would get. Grandpa, being good at reading the room, broke in and asked if we could all start having lunch. Here. On Sunday afternoons. He said that he loved seeing her happy and comfortable in her environment, and then Grandma mentioned she might like to start having her antiquing meetings at the inn. That is when I walked up. Apparently, I interrupted just before she could answer. Mom is relatively calmer by the end of her explanation.

"It's just, I have worked immeasurably hard. Now she thinks she can swoop in and claim credit for my success. Like I still need her." She groans and puts the pillow over her head.

"Okay, yes, it was wrong of Grandma to say all those things, but I think they may come from a semi-good place. Maybe this is the only way she knows how to be a part of your life." I'm grasping for straws.

"That's the problem. The only way she knows how to be in my life is to have some sort of control over it." She removes the pillow and sits up. "It's why I left in the first place."

I slink down next to her, unsure of what to say. She lies broken on the couch. This happens every time we see my grandparents. Maybe having them involved in our lives was a bad idea. Mom takes my silence as what it is and reassures me.

"Hey, don't worry about this. This is my own stuff. I think you should still try and build a relationship with them. Grandpa was excited about taking you golfing, and for him, the golf course is sacred ground. Take it as a huge compliment."

I know what she is trying to do. It's kind of working.

"He was probably just being nice." I shrug.

"No way. Anyone would want to spend time with you, even" she drags out the last word "golfing." This makes me laugh, and the mood is successfully lightened. I'm still worried about her though, so I suggest we stay in. Let the weekend manager finish the cleanup. We can sleep in then have breakfast in the morning and spend the whole day cuddling on the couch and make up for the movie night we missed. Everything else can wait.

# Chapter 20

I thought this week at school would be awkward, that Ben might act differently, but he hasn't. He hasn't mentioned our date either. What am I supposed to think? Does he not want to go anymore? Was I supposed to come find him after the wedding? The next day? Is he mad? He isn't acting mad.

By the time Thursday rolls around, I decide to call off the date. This is exactly the kind of distraction I didn't want. Marching into the Journalism room, bag in hand and speech prepared, I see him at our normal table with coffee ready. Mom's words ring in my ears: "Boys don't bring you coffee every day if they don't like you." I waver a little. No Amelia, you can do this.

When I approach our table Ben greets me "Good morning, Dorothy." He is in a good mood. Like a really good mood.

Normally his voice is a little hoarse in the mornings. It gives me pause, and I look around to make sure everything is okay. That is when I spot two tickets to the fall festival under my coffee cup. I freeze at the sight of them.

He didn't want to call off our date. I realize that I haven't said anything, and he is still smiling, clearly very proud of himself. "I've done some research." I sit on my stool, and he continues. "I know. I know. Research is your thing, but I can't go into this thing totally unprepared." He is inconceivably cute. "First, one must purchase tickets to this festival." I don't have the heart to tell him I get free tickets because Magnolia Manor always has a booth.

"Now I know that this is your town, and you probably know all the best booths and activities, but I asked around." he says. Asked who? I'm smiling like an idiot, and he takes it that he should continue. "I think our best bet is for me to pick you up at 5:30. I know that doesn't give us a lot of time after study session on Friday, but I heard the fried Oreos are the best at the beginning of the night." How does he know this?

"Okay. Stop." I catch his arm, and he flexes under my grip, causing my hand to tingle. I drop my hand. "Where are you getting all this information? And why haven't you mentioned this all week? I thought you didn't want to go anymore." He mocks horror and puts his hand to his heart.

"First, I don't ever reveal my sources. Second, I was planning. And third, you didn't bring it up either." He makes a fair point.

Picking up my coffee and taking a sip, I ponder his annoyingly excellent point. I didn't bring it up either. I pick up the tickets and stare at them. He would have had to go to a local business to get them, which means he either got them the day after the wedding or made a special trip. Point Ben. "Fair. We are really doing this?" I look up at him earnestly, and he grins a goofy grin.

"We are most definitely doing this" he confirms.

Class runs smoothly. My article was selected again, and Lisa had one selected too. The forecast says that the remainder of the day should have minimal passive aggression. It isn't until the end of class that the euphoria I have been feeling since I seeing the tickets is burst.

"I need to speak with you Amelia. You too Lisa." Mr. Bannerman announces as class dismisses for lunch. Lisa has not outright tried to assault me since the first week of school, however, makes it clear every single day she wants to. This can't be good for me. We glance at each other anxiously, and Ben whispers he will wait for me outside.

"Sir" we say in unison.

"Ladies, I have some good news" he starts. "As my top published writers, you two have been selected to join the senior journalism class at the Young Writers of America Conference at the end of term." I am taken aback. I thought only seniors got selected for that conference. As if he can read my mind he continues. "Normally this is an opportunity reserved for the seniors. However, you two have outranked several of the seniors, and I would be remiss in not recognizing that."

"Thank you" I say.

"Yes. Thank you." Lisa parrots, just as shocked as me.

"Now with that being said, part of your participation is that you both have to submit a series of articles to be sent in ahead of the conference. I want you to work on them together." We both attempt to interject but he continues sternly saying "Write a series. Your past articles share similar themes. Collaboration will be good for you."

I almost choke.

"Sir, I don't think— "Lisa begins.

"Now if either of you don't want to work together," he continues, "you both can decline. It would be a shame however if my top two choices for junior editors were not up to the challenge." No chance I am giving this up.

"No. We accept" I answer. I loop my arm around Lisa's and bring her toward me. She looks like I burned her but relaxes when I say, "We are thankful for this honor and won't let you down."

"Right," she says, patting my arm and squeezing. I grate my teeth but maintain composure.

"Good" he says clapping his hands together. "I'll email you both the information on the portal."

I nod my head and pull Lisa out of the room before she can go full mental breakdown on me. Ben and Kate, who have been obviously eavesdropping at the door, follow us.

"Okay before you say anything, don't." As I begin to speak she looks like her head might explode. Surprisingly, she relents. "We both want this opportunity and Mr.

Bannerman made it clear it is both of us or neither. Now, while I personally can't stand you and I'm sure the feeling is mutual; I'll admit you are a good writer. I'm willing to let that be the foundation for this partnership."

"Fine." she scoffs.

"That's it? No fight?" That was too easy.

"I obviously don't want to work with you either, but you're right. I don't want to miss out."

"Okay." I straighten my blazer. "Truce?"

"Yeah. Truce," she rolls her eyes.

Kate has now been joined by Bella, and Ben is staring at us. "What is happening?" he asks.

"I'll explain on the way to lunch," I respond. Not wanting to jinx anything that just happened, I walk away. I can hear Kate talking a mile an hour and Lisa taking a long huff, but it's progress. After thorough debriefing, Ben leaves me at the lunchroom. One day I'll ask him where he goes off too, but for now, it's pot-roast day.

# Chapter 21

I had plenty of time after study session to shower, attempt curls, not that the Georgia humidity will allow them to stay and put on some light makeup. Nothing much in case I sweat it off. The thing about fall in the south is it can still be 80 degrees in October. I'm hoping for 76 tonight. Completely ready to go, there is only one small hiccup. I have no idea what to wear. I've been staring at my closet for 20 minutes.

"Mia, are you ready to come down?" Mom calls from outside my door.

"I can't go." Sometimes I can be dramatic if I want. The door swings open and Mom laughs. She actually laughs.

"Hold on. I need my camera." She goes to find her phone.

"Mom, stop. What is so funny?" I whine.

"I just want to capture all your firsts, and not being able to decide on an outfit for a date is a big first." She says, her voice serious.

"Can you stop mocking me and come help?" I toss my hands up.

"Okay, calm down. You have done this before." She moves to look at my options and starts pulling things out.

"I have, but not with Ben and at school I never have to think about clothes. I'm always in a uniform. Private school has ruined me." I pout.

"I hadn't thought of that. Stunting you in fashion is unacceptable" she pauses rubbing her chin. "We will have to unenroll you immediately."

"Mom!"

"I'm kidding. Here." She hands me an outfit that I swear she pulled out of thin air: a pair of black flare pants I forgot I had and a thin emerald green baggy sweater. It is thin enough I won't be hot, but long sleeves so I won't be cold if the wind picks up later at night. "Hold please." She leaves my room and comes back with a long gold necklace and matching earrings.

"How?" I gape.

"How what?" she asks nonchalantly.

"For 20 minutes I tried. Then then you come in and in two minutes I have an outfit?"

"It's a gift," she shrugs. "Now get dressed. Your date will be here soon." She goes to the door then turning says, "Mia."

"Yeah?" I ask.

"Smile," and she snaps a picture of me standing in my pink bathrobe, outfit in hand, and bolts. I hear her laughing all the way out of the apartment.

Despite my mortification, I dress and am ready to go by 5:15. Unable to sit still, I head downstairs. I walk slowly in case Ben is one of those get there super early types. Plus, I want time to peek out one of the front windows. We didn't discuss logistics of whether he would pick me up out front or at the reception desk. Man am I nervous. Looking out the front window, I don't see him. Checking for his car I realize now; I don't know what Ben drives. Anytime he has walked me to the lot, I leave first.

"Boo!" I jump and scream. Ben is behind me, laughing, but catches me mid-panic attack.

"Why would you do that?" I mumble, holding my hand to my chest trying to steady my breath.

"I'm sorry, but you just looked so cute watching for me. I couldn't resist." He laughs.

"I wasn't watching for you," I grumble.

"No?" he questions.

"No. I was checking for guests." We both know I'm lying.

"Sure Dorothy." I look at him properly now. He is wearing jeans. I've never seen him in jeans. He has them paired with

143

a plain long sleeve navy tee. Blue is definitely his color. Butterflies flutter in my belly. He puts his hands in his pockets. "Shall we?"

"Yeah, sure." I'm really going to have to stop speaking in monosyllabic words if I want to get through this night.

Once we are out the front doors, Ben leads us to an old school blue truck. It stops me in my tracks. It has to be vintage. I don't know much about trucks, but it is some type of Ford. I think I would have noticed a truck like this in the school lot. "Wait. This is what you drive?" Like a gentleman, he moves to open the passenger door.

"Not usually, it's actually Brody's. He let me borrow it." He explains. I get in. Impressed.

"Nice touch." I comment. He closes the door and rounds the car. When he gets in, the curiosity has gotten the better of me. "Not that I'm complaining, but why did you have to borrow your brother's truck? What do you normally drive?"

"I drive a motorcycle." He waits for me to react. It isn't that surprising. Of course he does. "And I didn't think that your mom would, or any mom would love the idea of her daughter on the back of a motorcycle. So, I borrowed Brody's truck." He says waiting for my response.

"Very thoughtful, Benedict." I buckle in.

"Wait. Benedict. Are we back to that? Because I can go get the motorcycle." He panics.

"No, no." I laugh. "It was just such a gentlemanly move. I thought it called for your full name. Besides, you call me Dorothy, I need something else other than Ben to call you."

"Mhhh," he thinks, "that is an opening."

Tonight is going to be great. Any nerves have disappeared by the time we get to the event parking. Ben was right on the money getting the truck. One because my mom would have absolutely flipped had he shown up on a motorcycle, and two, the truck fits into the fall aesthetic. I feel like I'm in a country music video, but not in a bad way.

Event parking is in a cleared-out field lined with bales of hay. The festival itself is set up just off town by the Christmas tree farm. The family that owns the farm offered to host the festival when it got too big for the town square. It's still early and not quite dark yet, but I can still see the lights of the booths and entrance. Ben gets out and opens my door again. I've never had a boy open my door. Tyler sure didn't. That will be the last thought of him tonight, but it does make me feel better about letting my guard down.

Once I slide out of the truck, purse slung over my shoulder, Ben stops and looks a little awkward.

"You okay?" I question. Is he rethinking this? Is the country living already too much? Briarwood certainly doesn't have any cow fields.

"Yeah," he smiles, "but I want to ask you something." He does the classic hand-through-hair move that probably could get me to say yes to a lot of things. "Well, this is a date."

"Yes, we have confirmed that. Several times." I can't help but tease.

"Well, sometimes on dates, a guy and a girl might touch." Where is he going with this? I turn my head and look at him, and he quickly clarifies. "I mean all innocent. Like a guy might say put his arm around his date on a hayride or hold her hand as they walk through booths." Is Ben asking permission to hold my hand? He had no problem grabbing my face in Anatomy but asks to hold my hand. "Would this date fall into that category of dates, if it's not I am okay with that, but if it is..."

"It is." I don't have to think about it. The relief on his face is clear.

"Cool" this Ben is different. Normally he is confident and flirty but respectful date Ben is awkward, and it's melting my heart. "Lead the way, my lady." He gestures to the entrance, and I move ahead. He quickly matches my pace, and after a few more steps, slips his hand in mine. His hands are much larger than mine. I have to stretch my fingers, but it feels nice. This is already ranking high on my list of dates, and we haven't even gotten through the gates yet.

# Chapter 22

Benedict Blake is not cool, and I could not love it more. He is nerdy and sweet and fully into the festival experience. Not only have we sampled all the food booths, but I have also had the pleasure of watching Ben bob for apples despite my warning that they don't change the water. I've also seen him get cotton candy stuck around his mouth, which led to me wiping it away and nearly dying after. The festival is in full swing around us as Ben pulls me by the hand to line up for the hayride. He's like a little kid. If a little kid was 6ft tall.

"Slow down, little legs here" I plea. He stops and apologizes. Once in line, I catch my breath. I've smiled more tonight than I have in months. My cheeks hurt I have smiled so much. Ben shed some of his awkwardness and is a good mixture of his normal self but more carefree. It makes me wonder if, like me, he has to play a part at Briarwood. While we wait in line, Ben suggests we pick up our game of question and answer. Which he says is better than 20 questions because it never ends. We've played in almost every line. So far, all the questions have been simple. "What's your favorite color?" and such.

Ben rubs his chin. "I got one. What is your favorite movie?"

"No way. That is a terrible one!" I giggle. I'm literally a giggling schoolgirl.

"Why?"

"Because there are too many good movies to have a favorite" I protest.

"I see. Indecision. I will revise. What is your favorite type of movie?"

"Better. Mmmh. Old movies. Like really old, black and white movies, or 90s movies."

"Those aren't even close."

"Are too. What's your favorite?"

"Pretty Woman" he did not just say that. I am stunned out of laughter.

"No it isn't" I say.

"It is. I used to watch it with my mom. Julia Roberts is a national treasure" he isn't even a bit embarrassed.

"I can't believe you said that." Who is this guy? We get lost in each other's gaze until we have to move because the ride

148

worker starts to let people on the hayride. I'm so caught up in Ben I don't notice that it is Tyler's best friend Ian letting people on.

"Amelia?" Ian questions.

I jerk to look at him then awkwardly say, "Hey Ian."

"Hey. Long time no see." He looks Ben up and down then ignores him. "Tyler is around, he's been talking about you. He misses you."

"I'm sure." I am not letting this ruin my date. "Anyway, we better not hold up the line." I pull Ben onto the trailer loaded down with hay and move near the front. Once in our seats, he looks at me concerned.

"Tyler the non-boundary-respecting ex?" he asks. I nod my head affirming. "Wanna talk about it?"

"Nope" I say popping the p. Then I fix my attitude. I'm not upset with Ben. "I mean no. It's fine."

"I've been around Alyssa and Brody enough to know that 'it's fine' means it isn't," he puts an arm around me. "It's okay if you do want to talk about it, but I won't pry."

"I don't want to ruin our date."

"It won't." He reassures me.

"Okay." I stall "I told you it was a bad breakup, and it was. But Tyler seems to think eventually I'll forgive him. Sometimes he tries to text or call or ask Sarah Mae about me. She usually flips him off. Most of the time I can avoid the topic, but I still can't stand him." I take a breath. "The guy working the line is his best friend. The one downside of being in a small town, everyone knows everyone." I look to him to make sure I haven't freaked him out.

"We have confirmed he is an idiot but is it bad enough that you have something to worry about. Are you safe?" He is worried about my safety?

"He is dumb, not dangerous. It's just annoying. I blocked him and it's only out and about that I might run into him. Usually, I'm with my mom or Sarah Mae. He's scared of my mom and Sarah Mae is a good shield. When we broke up, she sent him a condolence card for his loss of me."

"I have to meet this Sarah Mae, but I can be your shield too, if you want." He looks sincere, and his comment implies that he will be around more.

"I think Briarwood is safe."

"Yeah, but I mean outside of Briarwood too."

"Oh" I take a moment for dramatic effect "I will be seeing you more outside of Briarwood?" Thoughts of Tyler fade away.

"Of course. I mean we do have a second date."

"Oh, we do."

"Yeah, I heard there is a winter carnival" Goofy Ben has reappeared.

The rest of the ride is perfect. The hayride goes out far enough from the festival that you can see the stars. I lean into Ben. With his arm wrapped around me, we stare up at the sky. Here under the stars, I'm totally happy. I feel like I belong here. This is the perfect moment in my own personal rom-com. Feeling very brave and before I can talk myself out of it, I turn to Ben and plant a soft kiss on his cheek. It says thank you for this night and that I very much can't wait for our second date. I just hope it's before the winter carnival.

# Chapter 23

Ben pulls into the inn's lot 30 minutes before my curfew. Mom has never really stuck to a curfew before, and as cool as she has been about the whole Ben thing, I think it was just her way of playing Mom a little. We sit silently in the truck. Up until now, I've never stared at my front porch longer. Finally, Ben breaks the silence.

"Tonight was fun," he says.

"It was." Not really clear of what to do, I move to open my door.

"Wait," Ben stops me and turns. "I mean, tonight was fun, but I don't really want it to be over yet."

"I agree," I blush.

His full body relaxes. "Maybe I can walk you inside?"

"Yeah, you can walk me inside." He is quick to exit the truck and run around to open my door. Once we make it up the steps, I don't hesitate in opening the door so we can enter the lobby. Inside, Ben asks, "We can hang out here or..." then it hits him. "Where do you stay?"

"Mom and I have a private apartment up the stairs, but actually, I have a better idea." Taking his hand, I lead him to the back porch.

I stop immediately because on the swing sits Tyler. Ben bumps into me and then moves his hands on both sides of me to steady me. "You okay?" he asks. I don't have time to respond before Tyler stands up to approach us.

"It's true. You moved on?" he spits. Tyler is tall but not as tall as Ben. His blonde hair is cut short. He's lankier than Ben too.

"Tyler, what are you doing here?" his entire presence irritates me.

"Ian texted me that you're on a date," he approaches us, and Ben pulls me next to him. Tyler stops. "I just thought it was kind of funny when you told me that you didn't want to date to focus on school."

"Maybe she just didn't want to date you," Ben has had time to fully assess the situation and looks beyond angry.

"I didn't ask you," Tyler snaps. Tyler doesn't realize that addressing Ben probably isn't good for his health.

"Okay. Stop." I say. "Both of you." I place a hand on Ben's arm, then nod to him that I am fine. He looks down at me and relaxes but only a little.

"Tyler, you and I both know I didn't break up with you just because I was going to Briarwood. You were the one that couldn't handle that."

"Come on Mia. I said I was sorry. I overreacted. I promised I wouldn't pressure you anymore" Tyler tries to come closer, and I think Ben does actually growl. I hold my hand up.

"No. We have had this conversation. You didn't respect me or any boundaries I set. Then you used me leaving for school to try to get me to waiver. When it didn't work, we broke up," as I speak, I can feel Ben tense next to me. No one has a good reaction to the reason for our breakup. However, Ben has a bit of a protective side and I need to get him calm.

"So what? You just replace me with this guy? You think some rich kid from Briarwood is going to treat you better than me?" he says exasperated.

Ben must be exercising some serious self-control because he lets me answer. "This is Ben. Ben is my-"

"Boyfriend," I choke at his words, but I don't correct him. He takes my hand and pulls me behind him. "And I don't really like the idea of some guy showing up on my girlfriend's porch, especially since it's clear he isn't wanted."

"Look man, maybe you can take a step back. Amelia and I have known each other for a while." Tyler says stepping forward.

"Yeah, and clearly you left a bad taste." Ben doesn't let up. Instead he meets Tyler and towers over him. As Ben glares down at Tyler, I feel the heat roll off of him. When he clenches his fists, I step in between them.

"Enough. Leave Tyler." I demand. I've had enough.

"Fine. I'll go." Tyler walks to the door then turns to say "Call me when you realize that he only wants one thing." Ben goes to follow him, but I grab his hand pulling him back. Tyler leaves tail tucked. I have to lean on the wall next to me. Ben comes to stand in front of me and rubs his hands up and down my arms.

"I'm sorry if I overstepped" he says then takes a deep breathe. I look up at him shocked.

"Wait. What?" I look into his stormy eyes "My ex shows up and tries to ruin the end of our date, and you're apologizing to me?"

"Amelia, you didn't ask him here. It was clear you didn't want him here. You have nothing to be sorry about," it breaks me. Here is this guy who I have spent almost every day with, being polite, and asking to hold my hand, and handling my ex showing up better than anyone in history probably would, and being perfect, and I lose all sense.

I lean up on my tiptoes, surprising Ben and myself, and I kiss him. I have to steady myself by placing a hand on his shoulder, but the moment my lips touch his, he grabs my waist, holding me in place. It lasts only a moment, then I lower down and stare up at him.

"Thank you," I blush.

"You're welcome." He releases me. "Anyway, before we were interrupted, you had an idea."

"Yeah, I, um, well, I wanted to sit on the swing with you and watch for fireflies. It's rare this time of year, but sometimes they are still out, but it feels kind of tainted now."

"I understand. Do you want me to go?"

"No, but maybe we can sit in the sunroom instead." I pause before we head in. "Ben, why did you tell Tyler you were my boyfriend?"

"Honestly, he didn't seem like he would back off if I didn't."

"Oh, okay." I start toward the door, but he catches my hand.

"I mean, as far as I'm concerned, he can keep thinking it. Other people can think it too," his face is earnest. He's asking without asking and I can't breathe.

"Other people?" I ask.

"All the people" he looks at me sheepishly.

"Okay." I leave him speechless on the porch and walk inside. I appear more confident than I am because on the inside, I'm freaking out. I think I just agreed to be Ben's girlfriend.

# Chapter 24

## End of November

Dating Ben is strange. It isn't strange in a way that it's cause for alarm. It's strange in the way that it's the complete opposite of anything I ever experienced with Tyler. I know that it's wrong to compare when I have a limited number of samples. However, comparison is a journalistic staple. With Tyler, we had fun. However, my initial attraction to him, as bad as it seems, is that he showed interest. No boy had ever called me pretty or asked me out on a date. It was nice to feel wanted. My advanced intelligence had not caught up to the social awareness needed to discern a douchebag.

Almost a year of experience with a subpar partner and now about a month and a half of dating an honest-to-goodness good guy has given me perspective. Tyler was immature, selfish, and DUMB. How did I not realize he was so unforgivably dumb? Most of our conversations surrounded town events, recent movies, or other people from high school. Sure, going to basketball games to watch him play or dates to the local theater was fun, but it was all surface level.

Dating Ben is like finding my intellectual equal. We get into full debates over the topics of my articles. Sometimes I think he actually agrees with me but just wants to play devil's advocate to get me flustered. We went on a date to an art museum for crying out loud! In all fairness, I think he was trying to impress Sarah Mae. The date was the result of her calling him uncultured when he commented on a video she was watching. It was about an artist who had been building sculptures out of trash at recycling centers to protest how much goes to waste.

I thought it would be the end for him, but then he suggested a group excursion to a new museum a few towns over. Sarah Mae relented that he may not be completely uncultured but that is only be because he surprised us all by showing the director some of her art. Now she has an up-and-coming spotlight at the museum. I think it is exactly what the Spice Girl's meant if you want to get with me you have to get with my friends.

We spend time with our families too. What is that? Tyler never wanted to do a movie night with my mom. He always wanted our dates to be alone. Hindsight and all of that. I have learned recently that family is incredibly important to Ben. His mom was diagnosed with breast cancer a little over a year ago. They found it too late, and it had progressed. He was incredibly broken up about it, which led to some issues he hasn't really gone into detail about. With that being said. The Ben lunchtime mystery has been solved.

He goes home.

To have lunch with his mom.

You have got to be kidding me! Not only does he surpass Tyler in range of intellect, but also has an advanced emotional intelligence that cannot be normal for the typical teenage boy to possess. So here we are in the dining room on a Friday afternoon with his mom, Alyssa, and a deck of cards playing spades. While it feels like I'm winning in every other aspect of my life right now, I'm not at cards.

Alyssa and Grace have to be cheating. They've won three straight games.

"That's it. I give up. I'm going back to school because clearly that's the only place I'll have success in my life." I say slapping my cards down.

Ben, an equally sore loser, says, "Seriously, are there hidden mirrors somewhere?" He winks at me.

Grace, the ever-gracious winner, responds, "Oh now, you two may not be out for taking Vegas by storm, but I'm sure you'll win a hand eventually." Alyssa laughs.

"I'll take my loss as usual, with a to-go cup of coffee mixed with a scoop of shame. Thank you ladies, it's been fun." I stand, partially sore we lost. Again. Also, partially because I have to go meet Lisa to finalize our article submissions for the conference. That whole situation has been going as well as it can. The girl is abrasive at best. I do have to give it to her; she can write.

"Oh, come now, one more game," Alyssa pleads, smiling because in the sweet interior is a fiend when it comes to playing cards.

Ben saves the day, "No, we really do have to get back to campus." He rounds the table and kisses his mom on the head. He's delicate and sweet with her. However, their interactions are always laced with an unsaid sadness. The doctors gave her 6 months. It isn't something Ben likes to talk about. It's the reason he's desperate to come home every day.

We're out the door and pulling off in Brody's truck that he lets Ben drive permanently. I'm sure that the classic truck isn't meant to have as much mileage as Ben has put on it driving back and forth from Magnolia Manor and Briarwood. According to Alyssa, Brody is willing to make the sacrifice to see Ben happy.

"Tell me, what is the war plan for today?" Ben asks as we turn onto the road.

"I don't need a war plan to meet with Lisa. We're just finalizing the submission packet," I roll my eyes.

"Oh sure. So that wasn't the two of you that got into such a heated argument over font size that freshmen ran from the library in terror?"

"It was a disagreement and we handled it." I shrug.

"You know, I'm starting to think you like arguing with her. It's like some weird form of anger management you have," his analysis isn't unfounded. As much as I hate to admit it, working with Lisa does make me angry, but it's also cathartic. Don't get me wrong. We are far from friends. More frenemies.

"It'll be fine." I assure him.

"Well, as much as I don't trust that and would love to play referee, I have an appointment with the counseling department. Can you manage not to kill her without me?" I know he's kidding, but if I asked, he would come with me to the library and sit while we worked.

"I promise. I'll refrain from homicide." I pretend to pout resting my elbow on the door's armrest.

"Good girl" he smirks. I look out the window so he can't see me blushing.

# Chapter 25

Ben leaves me at the library door. I take a deep breath. Today will be fine. Thus far, Lisa and I have managed to work together without injury and only two warnings from Mr. Bannerman. We've learned after our last altercation that our best bet is to reserve one of the soundproof study rooms. The librarian was hesitant at first, but was willing to risk it to prevent us from being any more disruptive than we already have been the last month.

I'm a little early, so there is a good chance I will be able to beat Lisa to the room and get my pick of seats. Which will bother her just enough to start the afternoon off with a bang. I quietly move through the library toward the back hallway that leads to the study rooms. As I pass by, some of the doors are open and some closed with "do not disturb" signs. Midterms have already passed, but there's always some sort of test or project to prepare for, and it isn't uncommon to see many of the rooms occupied. Especially on Fridays.

Approaching the door to our reserved room, I notice the door is closed. Ugh. Lisa beat me here. Which means she will be sitting in the chair facing the door looking all smug. I sling the door open, ready to meet her condescending face. Instead, I'm greeted with her back. I can't see her face because it's attached to Bella's face. I hit my knee on a chair and groan, the two break apart. Not sure what to do, I mutter an apology and shut the door behind me.

I had no clue that they were dating. Now that I think of it, it makes sense. They are always together. Lisa's only nice to Bella. I guess I can see it, but from the way they separated, I don't think it is public knowledge. Suddenly the door flings back open, and a panicked Bella leaves head down past me, and I'm being pulled by my collar into the room by a surprisingly strong Lisa.

"You didn't see anything" she tells me sternly. "You didn't see anything, and you can't tell anyone" Lisa panics. I don't think I have ever seen Lisa afraid of anything. She is fear. Clarity hits me.

"I don't know what you're talking about" I say setting my bag down on the table.

Lisa on the verge of tears continues, "You don't understand. You can't have seen anything. If our parents find out—" I can't believe I actually feel sorry for Lisa. So much about how she carries herself and pushes people around makes sense now.

"Listen, I won't tell anyone." I interject. "As far as I'm concerned, I was standing outside, and a crazy lady pulled me into a study room." I want to say more. I want to comfort her. I want to tell her she shouldn't hide who she is.

She sits across from me and stares at me for a long time. I stare back to convince her of the truth.

"I'm not embarrassed if that's what you think, of liking Bella, I mean. It's just my parents are strict, and so are hers, and well it's—"

"The south." I finish her sentence. "Yeah. I know, and that sucks."

"It does?" she seems surprised.

"It isn't my business. You know, what you do or choose to share with other people. But yeah, it sucks that you have to hide a part of you. That you have to be afraid for people to see." I explain.

"Why are you being nice to me?" she asks. I wonder the same thing.

"To be honest, I'm not sure. You are the living worst" I laugh. "But just because you tried to get me to drop out and go back to what was it, 'my podunk town', doesn't mean that you should ever worry about something this monumental."

"I'm not sure if I hate you more or less now," she is brutally honest.

"Let's hope it's the latter," I say.

164

"I think it might be," and then the sign of the world ending appears, and Lisa smiles at me.

"So your parents..." I choose my next question carefully "They don't know?"

Lisa takes a deep breath before responding. "They know. The signs were there when I was younger. Barbie always kissed Barbie and never Ken. I refused to be a debutante. My parents and I have an understanding. As long as it stays private, it's fine. But if it ever becomes public. If I embarrass them..." her voice breaks. "I'm not their daughter anymore".

"Lisa, no. That's terrible. A parent's love should never be conditional." Suddenly, I'm angry for her and not at her.

"It's why I work so hard. At school. On the paper. To make up for the fact I'm such a disappointment." She wipes her eyes on the corner of her sleeve.

Talk about getting an expose. School Terror is Terrified: One girl's story of resilience in a world where parents suck. The desire to comfort her is overwhelming. "Lisa, I'm not just telling you this because I'm incredibly uncomfortable with the amount of emotion you're showing and I feel like I have seen behind the Wizard's red curtain. But you are not a disappointment. You are brilliant and strong. If your parents can't get over whatever archaic presumptions they have about who you should be, the hell with them."

She takes what I say in "So what now? You like me all of a sudden? I've been terrible to you".

"I understand you now, and if we're sharing today, I do like working with you. In a masochistic kind of way." I say trying to lighten the mood.

"I'm sorry, Amelia."

"For what?"

"For being so awful. You didn't deserve it."

"No, I didn't, but I forgive you."

"Just like that?"

"Yeah, just like that."

We are able to get through the rest of the afternoon with no arguments. Well, no screaming matches. We finished the packet, and both sent copies at the same time to Mr. Bannerman. It's actually kind of brilliant. Since it's an election year, we chose to explore the effects of word of mouth on teens and children. Finding things kids say and repeat at school and tracking it back to the original source.

A series of 10 articles that help show the dangers of repeating information without fact-checking. The final article gives tips on finding legitimate sources and fact-checking information. We even created a website link in the school blog to help people register to vote. Given most students at the school are under the voting age, we decided that the topic was still worth it because it gives good information to parents and students. It's also non-biased as we used rumors from both major parties for examples.

Now we just have to sit back and wait for Mr. Bannerman's approval. While packing up, a knock at the door has us both turning our heads. We aren't left guessing long when Kate and Bella enter. Bella's eyes are red, and Kate looks determined.

"Can I talk to Amelia?" Kate asks, locking her gaze on me. "Alone."

Lisa responds, "It's fine, I handled it."

Kate looks at her momentarily hostile but then says determined, "I still want to talk to her."

"It's okay," I say.

Bella and Lisa leave, and I notice Lisa nodding at me as they exit. Kate closes the door. Suddenly I feel like a cornered mouse.

"Here's the thing, I know you saw something interesting and I know that Lisa has done absolutely nothing to earn any grace in your book, but Bella is sweet and innocent. She doesn't deserve to be hurt by anyone. Understand?" Kate is a good sister. It's too bad she doesn't realize I'm not a threat.

"You don't have to worry Kate. I already told Lisa, but I will tell you too, I'm not going to tell anyone what I saw. It isn't my business." I try to make sure I say it clear enough she understands.

"I need more than that. I don't think you understand the gravity of the situation. Our parents are crazy religious. Like, we have money for our religion crazy religious. If they find out, they'll send Bella away. Do you want that on your conscience?" She talks fast, and I can see she really is afraid.

167

"I won't because I'm not going to tell anyone. Listen, I think that Bella and Lisa shouldn't have to hide anything, but I'm not going to out them. Besides, if anything else I understand Lisa better now, and want to see her implode less." Kate takes in what I say.

"Is this how they grow all the girls in Windy Creek?" she questions. "Because a Briarwood girl would have already posted on one of the secret Instagram pages."

"Briarwood has secret Instagram pages?" First I'm hearing of it.

"Do you not have social media?" she asks, getting off topic.

"Not really?" I shrug.

"We'll have to fix that. I knew I liked you Bedelia. We are going to be really good friends from now on, you and me." She comes over and puts her arm around me and gives me a squeeze.

"Is that just so you can keep an eye on me to make sure I don't spill any secrets?" I ask uncomfortably.

"Yes and no." she smiles. "Besides, you can't spend all your time with Ben."

I don't spend all my time with Ben. Do I?

# Chapter 26

"Run it by me one more time. Kate invited you to a party?" Ben asks as he tosses a pillow up and down on the couch in our small apartment. I'm in my room looking through my closet. Mom has laid out some pretty clear rules. Ben and I can be alone in the apartment as long as we stay in the living room. If at any time he enters my room, she'll come in, sit us down, and make us watch old school health class videos on VHS. I'm not sure where she intends to find a VHS player, but I never doubt the capabilities of Lizzie Roberts.

"She invited US to a party," I peek my head out, "and WE are going."

"I don't get it though. She just randomly up and invites you to a party, and you say yes. You don't want to hang out with Briarwood kids" Ben's argument is not wrong. I can't exactly tell him that I want to go to the party to ensure Kate, Bella, and I guess Lisa, that I won't spill what I saw. Plus, after our talk, Kate made the excellent point that I don't really hang out with anyone or haven't attempted to make any friends outside of Ben. I've had no interest in the matter. I really don't want to tell him now I'm worried that I've become a little too focused on him. I tend to have a one-track mind. First, it was establishing myself academically. Once I accomplished that, Ben.

"I hang out with you." I point out.

He stands and crosses the room without coming too close to my door. "Yeah, but as established, I'm the exception," he retorts smirking.

"I know. You are the only exception," I sigh, pulling out a sweater dress. "And while I like the way things are going, I'm a little worried." As soon as the words leave my lips, the mood shifts. Fear flashes across Ben's face.

"Worried about us?" He is quick to respond.

I abandon the dress on my bed and leave my room. We need to have this conversation face to face. "I'm not worried about us. I like the way things are going with us. I'm really happy."

"But?"

"But Kate pointed out that I only spend time with you. I haven't made any friends unless you count Lisa, and I don't think collaborative yelling matches equals friendship." I can see he wants to come up with a quick response, but the benefit of Ben is he's always considerate.

"Friends are overrated." Or not.

"Ben," I plea.

"I guess I get what you are saying, and while I'd like to think I am enough to satisfy all your intellectual needs, I've seen how you look forward to working with Lisa. You need school friends. I get it. But a party?"

"I have to start somewhere," I shrug and give him a quick kiss before turning back to my room.

"Can't you join a book club? You like to read." He crashes back on the couch, and I hear the cushions puff from my room.

"Do you not want to go to the party? Rumor is it before you started dating me you went to a lot of them." I didn't mean it like that. But the silence that came after I said it made it loud and clear I said the wrong thing.

I peer out of my room, seeing Ben with his head down. I cross the room and stand in front of him lifting his head. "Ben?"

"I have to tell you something." Ben's voice sounds with defeat. My senses go on high alert. I know Ben. My Ben. The version of him I have seen in private conversations and with his family. However, just because I haven't made friends at Briarwood doesn't mean I don't hear things. Or that Kate didn't show me posts on the secret Instagram pages. I had a vague idea that Ben use to be wild, nevertheless surely it can't be that bad.

The way he is looking up at me tells me different. His eyes are full of... shame. His regret is evident before he even speaks. "Before my mom, I was different. I partied a lot. I was drinking and cutting school and hanging out with people I shouldn't have been. If you googled entitled rich kid, my picture was the first result. I didn't take anyone's feelings into account." He pauses then takes a breath. "Then I found out about Mom's cancer. You'd think that would've been enough to set me straight, but it wasn't." I can see he is scared to continue.

"Go on," I encourage.

"At the end of last year, I got really drunk with a couple of guys, and we broke into the headmaster's office." Ben the Burglar.

"Okay. I'm assuming that ended poorly," I say still processing.

"Yeah, obviously we got caught. My dad was livid, but Mom was heartbroken. It was on a treatment day, and she was already weak. Having to stand in front of her sobering up snapped something in me. I'd been selfish. Thinking only about how upset I was that I would lose her that I didn't even think about what she was going through. Then here I was making it worse."

My eyes tear up as he explains. He looks broken. "Ben."

"No, don't pity me. I deserved every bit of trouble I had coming. Dad was mad enough that he was going to send me away to boarding school, but Brody begged him not to. I didn't know then that the doctors hadn't given Mom much time. That we were literally fighting for time. Dad worked it out with the headmaster that I wouldn't be expelled as long as I cleaned up my act, and I had to participate in the mentor program."

It takes me a minute to process all of this information. Ben getting expelled. Is he only on good behavior to avoid being sent away? Where does that leave us? Our relationship? We are only together because he was my mentor. Forced proximity. The Ben I know has done nothing but live up to all his family obligations. Am I an obligation? A part of him cleaning up his act? Dating the nice girl?

"Hey, I see those wheels turning, and I have a few guesses on what you're thinking, and the answer is no. To all of it." He grabs my face.

"No?"

"No, I'm not only different because I have to be. No, I'm not only here because I don't want to get sent away."

"Mind reader, are you?"

"Amelia, I know you. I've spent the last three months trying to learn everything I can about you. You have been my bright spot in all of this mess." He stands and pulls me in for a hug. I instinctively wrap my arms around him. "I'm not proud I messed up, but I'm glad I did. I'm different now. I needed to change. I needed to see all the things I was taking for granted. It makes me appreciate everything I have now." He is respectably honest.

"Thank you for telling me." I pull back and look up at him. "I know it wasn't easy. I'm glad you are the you, you are now." I really am.

He smiles down at me. "Yeah."

"Yeah," I give him a quick kiss.

"Does that mean that we don't have to go to this party? Lizzie and Amelia movie night?" He sounds hopeful.

"We don't have to go if you don't want to." After what he shared, I don't want to put him in an atmosphere he won't be comfortable in.

"Amelia, do you want to go? Because we can, you know. I'm not an addict, I'm not at risk of falling into old habits. I just don't enjoy the party scene anymore. But if you want to go, I would rather I be the one to take you then Kate." Why is he perfect?

"I don't really want to go, but I feel like I owe Kate," I sigh.

"Yeah, I don't get it, but we can still go. Besides, there are some benefits to parties."

"I'm listening."

"I can dance with you." And just like that, all is restored in the universe. My heart swells, and I feel like I am closer to Ben now than I was before.

# Chapter 27

Ben was wrong. Well, he was right, but he was wrong. Okay, let me explain. There is no dancing. There is loud music, and I'm sure at one time there may have been dancing. However, by the time Ben and I arrive at the party, things are a mess. The party that Kate insisted I come to in an attempt to expand my social circle is in a mansion near the country club. Apparently, some kid's parents are out of the county, and he decided to celebrate by having the entire junior and senior classes over. Our school is smallish, but the number of people overwhelms the space. Ben and I make it through the door, and regret hits me instantly. Suddenly, my chest is tight, and I feel like I can't breathe.

Locked hand in hand, Ben navigates us through the crowd in what I assume is the main living space until we reach a door leading to a patio. Outside is better. There's a huge pool that could be at a resort. The area is littered with teenagers. Some on loungers, others standing along the edges of walls huddled into circles laughing. I take a minute to breathe fresh air. It's a cool night, but not so much that it's uncomfortable.

"You okay?" Ben asks. "We don't have to stay."

"I'm fine. It's just a lot." I've never been anxious. At least not the medical definition of it. I have normal anxiety when trying new things, but this is a different kind of anxious. Everything around me is unfamiliar. I try to find recognition on some of the faces but can't find any. My stomach is in knots.

Ben leads us over to an empty lounger set, and we sit down. "Thoughts?"

"This is a Briarwood party?" I ask, looking around.

"Pretty much. Why? What were you expecting?" He takes one hand in his and then uses his other to draw circles on my knee. It's soothing.

"I don't know. Sophisticated music. Virgin sacrifices?" I realize in the moment all of my information about parties has come from movies.

"Nope, just a bunch of kids drinking and trashing someone's house. Sometimes there's beer pong."

"Mmh," it's all incredibly dull. I'm not really sure what I thought would happen. "Should I try to find Kate?"

As if she could predict my statement, I hear her. "Amelia Bedelia, you came." She plops on the same lounger as me and almost falls over.

"I did." I scan her over. She's wearing a too-short-for-this-weather long sleeve dress that's a shade of green I can't place. Her hair is kind of a mess.

"You came too late" she pouts. "All the fun is done." Something's off with her. I mean other than her obvious drunkenness.

"Kate, are you feeling okay?" I have to lean her up a little.

"Oh, I'm great. I have a secret too. It's a big one, it's as big the one you know. Wanna hear?" she slurs.

"Secret?" Ben perks up behind me.

"Not now" I chastise. "Kate, I don't think now is a good time to tell any secrets. Why don't we see if we can find you some water?"

"There's water over there." Kate slings herself around to point to the pool, and then Ben jumps into action, stopping us all from falling over.

"No, Kate, I don't think you want that water," he says. "Amelia, we need to get her inside."

"Obviously," we both stand and each takes a side of a very giggly Kate.

As we stabilize her, Lisa and Bella come barreling out of the house. They spot us and come over. "Kate is drunk," Bella says. This is the first time I've heard her speak a complete sentence.

"I gathered that," I say, earning me a glare from Lisa.

"Boooooo! Here comes the party police." Kate whines in our arms. "I don't need you guys, Ben and Amelia BEDEEILLIA can keep me company now. You two can go enjoy all your alone time. I know how much you like that."

I watch as Bella and Lisa bristle, so I break in "Okay Kate. How about we get you out of here."

"We can't take her back to our house. Our parents will flip" Bella says. Bella and Kate's relationship is fascinating. I momentarily wonder what it would be like to have a sibling.

"She can't come home with me either" Lisa says. "My dad is home and he's a light sleeper." Eyes turn to me.

"I can take her. My mom might flip, but at least she'll be safe" I offer. Ben looks at me like I have three heads. It only takes one visual plea for him to relent.

"Come on. Help me get her to the truck" he groans. He really is the best.

"Yah! Sleep over with my new best friend! See Bella, I have friends. You have Lisa and I have Bediela." Kate runs her hands through my hair as she talks, and Ben, clearly over it, picks her up and carries her to the door.

We follow suit. It takes me, Lisa, and Bella calming and coaxing to get her in the truck. I get Bella's number to text her when we are safely home. She apologizes profusely. She assures me Kate never gets drunk, that something set her off. Well, if my wish was to make a new friend, I have succeeded after tonight.

After a very long drive back to Windy Creek, we finally arrive back at Magnolia Manor. It is only after stopping at Taco Bell to prevent Kate from trying to leap out of the truck. I officially never want to go to a party again, and I was barely there. Ben is angry too. I think mostly at Kate but maybe me too. I don't blame him. We should have had the movie night.

We somehow manage to get Kate up and into my room without disturbing any guests. How I don't know because when she saw we were at an inn, she began making inappropriate comments about the three of us getting a room. Mom also wasn't in the apartment. It's strange because normally she'd be waiting up. I'm home well before I said I would be. She might be out to dinner.

Ben and I manage to get Kate in my bed and tucked in. I think mom will forgive the no Ben in my room rule being broken. The drunk girl will distract her. God, what was I thinking bringing Kate here? I put a trash can by the bed and grab a bottle of water from the fridge. She will need it.

Ben plops down on the couch and puts his hands over his eyes. I approach him carefully.

"Sooooo, fun party." I attempt at breaking the tension.

"So fun," he deadpans.

"Ben, I'm really sorry. We shouldn't have gone. Please don't be mad." I sit next to him and he lifts himself up.

"You think I'm mad at you?"

"Kinda? You were quiet on the ride back. It was pretty obvious you were angry."

"I'm not mad Amelia. I'm upset, and not at you."

"Upset?"

"Yeah, at myself. I knew that party would be like that. Then when we got there, the look on your face. I shouldn't have let you go. I should've insisted we stayed here or taken you out." He takes my hand. "Parties are nothing but trouble. Clearly from how Kate is passed out in your bed right now. That is my old life, and I don't want you around that. It isn't safe."

I realize I'm smiling. I realize it's weird that I'm smiling. "You were upset because you wanted to keep me safe?"

"Yeah silly." He pokes my forehead, pushing me back on the couch. "I care about you."

"I care about you too." My stomach does the little flutter thing it does every time Ben says something Ben-ish.

"Well, I'm glad we have that settled" he leans back next to me on the couch.

"I'm a little disappointed" I say. "I was promised dancing."

"Oh, I can fix that." He is on his feet quicker than I can process, pulling his phone from his pocket. The next thing I know, music is playing. I recognize the song from to the wedding playlist.

"May I have this dance?" Ben bows to me.

"Of course," I giggle. Ben swoops me into his arms. That's how we spend the night. Slow dancing in my living room with my drunk friend passed out in the room next to us. This is way better than any party.

181

"You went to your first party ever and left 15 minutes after you got there to take care of a drunk classmate?" Mom pauses, then continues "Then, you bring that drunk classmate here instead of to her house, and now she's sleeping in your bed, and you're making her breakfast?" Mom stares at me as she sips her coffee from a barstool opposite of me.

"You left out the part where I came home with my boyfriend to an empty apartment which made getting her in here unnoticed easier," I say as I scoop eggs onto a plate where an already warm tortilla and some sausage lay. Kate seemed pleased with her Taco Bell last night, leading me to infer a breakfast taco would be just the key. "Want to fill in the gap of why you got home past curfew?"

"I was out" Mom grins, leading me to believe she was on a date. "Besides, we aren't talking about me. Should I be worried about you? So far this year the only people from school I've met are your boyfriend and a girl who got drunk at a party. I mean, I am glad that you chose to come here, and Ben is great, but I'm still worried about your social life."

"I don't know. I have Ben, and I'm friendly with the kids in journalism. I'm just not really interested in hanging out with the other kids outside of school. From what little I saw at the party, I don't think I have much in common with them. Plus, I have Sarah Mae and you. How many friends does one person really need?"

"As long as you are okay. And the drunk girl?" Mom motions to my door.

"Her name is Kate. We have a couple classes together. Well, her and her twin. I'm not really sure what happened to her before Ben and I got there. She was fine earlier at school." I put all the breakfast items on a tray, grabbing some Tylenol from the medicine cabinet.

Mom gets up to refill her coffee cup. "I trust you to make good choices, Mia, just be careful who you surround yourself with."

"I will. According to her sister, this isn't typical. Something happened." I reassure her.

"Okay. Take Drunkella her breakfast. I'm going to head downstairs to give you girls some space. Come get me if you need me."

"Thanks." Mom gives me a hug and a kiss on the forehead then heads out. I go into my room to wake Kate. At the sound of the door, a very disheveled Kate groans. "I don't care what time it is Bella, I will murder you."

"Not Bella," I come closer to the bed. Kate attempts to sit up unsuccessfully then takes in her surroundings.

"Bedelia." Her voice is hoarse. "It's coming back to me. Are we in a library?" She sits up and looks around the room.

"No, this is my room. Ben and I brought you back here last night. Bella asked me to. You were... a lot." I set the tray down.

"Thanks." she repositions herself and stares at the tray. Her face goes a little green. "I don't think I can eat this."

"It's okay, but maybe try some of the water." I sit on the edge of the bed as she nods and takes a tentative sip. "Do you want to talk about it?"

"About what Bedelia? My lack of ability to hold my liquor. Thought that was pretty clear." She says evasively.

"I know we haven't known each other long, but that wasn't it. I won't push, but if you want to talk about it, I'm here." I offer. Kate sighs and for a long minute pauses.

"I guess you already have one twin's secret. You might as well have the other." She takes a long draw of her water. "You aren't the only one who saw something you shouldn't Friday." She closes her eyes. "I saw my dad with his receptionist."

I try to still my face but shock hits me. "When you say you saw them?"

"I walked in on them mid-act, Amelia, and apparently there isn't enough alcohol in the world that can burn that image from my brain."

"Does Bella know?"

"No, and I can't tell her. It would break her. My parents make a huge deal about being the perfect Christian family unit. Bella is so worried about disappointing them, but my dad is just a huge hypocrite." Anger. That is the emotion in her voice.

"What happened after you... you know?"

"My dad chased me down and made me swear not to tell my mom. Promised me anything I want. A car. A summer trip to Europe. Like it's that easy, just to buy me. I don't want this secret, and going to Paris won't change that." She shakes her head.

"What are you going to do?" I ask.

"I don't know. Part of me wants to tell my mom. She deserves to know. I just don't want to be the reason our world blows up." Tears start to slip from her eyes.

"You aren't, though. The reason your world will blow up. Your dad is. It isn't fair for him to make you lie for him." I want her to believe me. I'm angry for her, and a little grateful I don't have a dad to put me in a situation like this.

"I hate him, Amelia." Her face looks like a little kid. Innocent. Small. Too small to handle the burden she has been saddled with.

"That's fair."

"You know, you are a pretty good friend. I'm sorry Lisa gave you such a tough time at the beginning of the year." She says wiping her eyes.

"That's what Lisa said yesterday. It's okay. All of you are going through a lot." I say in attempt at consoling her.

"That we are, but it doesn't make anything that we have done okay. Lisa bullying you, me getting drunk. It's no way to handle things. You really are a good person Bedelia and a good friend." Kate says. "I should head out. Bella is probably losing it."

"I can drive you." I offer.

"Thanks, Bedelia. For everything."

"Anytime." I respond "But maybe next time we hang out, we skip the drinking."

"I like that plan."

I go downstairs to let Mom know I'm driving Kate home. I gave her a few details about Kate's situation. I don't think it counts as breaking Kate's trust. Mom said I could let her know she is welcome to stay if she needs to. I knew something had upset Kate, but I never imagined it was the magnitude it was.

Kate was talkative on the way to her house. I think mostly just to calm her nerves. When we got to her house, Bella was outside waiting, worry on her face. I told Kate to call if she needed to talk or if her and Bella wanted to crash at our house after she talked with her mom. She promised she would.

I call Ben as I'm leaving. He was more than happy to come meet me at a coffee shop around the corner. He had a lot of questions, but I told him I couldn't break Kate's trust. He only pouted up until I promised him a makeup date. We decided to have a movie night in. I love how Ben has managed to fit into my life so well. It's getting to the point that it's hard to imagine doing things without him. The thought scares me.

# Chapter 29

Any concerns about my social life being in danger have been washed away. To Ben's dismay, I've developed a full-blown friendship with Kate, Bella, and Lisa. He isn't upset I have friends, just that he has to share my time.

Kate did tell her mom, and as expected, it blew up her household. Apparently, her dad tried to blame her, and her mom kicked him out. According to Kate, her mom suspected it for a while and was relieved she had proof. She also said that her dad is pissed because in her parents' prenup, it stated her mom would get everything if he cheated. Now her dad is in a tiny little apartment near his office with not a single leg to stand on.

Bella took it better than Kate expected. From what I have gathered, their dad is kind of an ass. Okay, not kind of. He is an ass that has been making the three of them miserable for years. The rumor mill at school was the worst of it, but it died down after a few weeks. Lisa's ability to scare anyone who mentioned it came in handy. It's how we all got to be surprisingly close.

Now it's close to the end of term, and Lisa and I are gearing up to go to Atlanta for the Young Writers of America Conference. Our packet was not only accepted but chosen to represent the school over all the senior submissions. I thought the paper's senior editor was going to block us both from getting any more articles published when Bannerman announced it, but he was actually impressed. It helps that he got early acceptance to Yale. We are small potatoes at this point.

Kate, Lisa, Ben, and I are sitting at a table in the back of the Journalism room, waiting for the bell to ring. The sound of printers behind us.

"Let's talk plans for next weekend. I know you two are going to be honed into the conference all this weekend, so we need to celebrate your success next weekend" Kate says.

"Don't you think planning to celebrate could jinx us?" I ask as Ben sits next to me and plays with a loose curl. I love December. It's the best time of the year, less humidity, which means my hair will hold curls.

"Nonsense" Kate waves me off. "The hard work is done. All you have to do now is present."

"Yeah, just talk in front of hundreds of people. No big deal." I roll my eyes.

Lisa chimes in, "I can do the bulk of the talking if you're nervous." Of course, she would love that.

"No, I can do it." I narrow my eyes at her.

189

"Don't start." Ben interjects. "I cannot sit through another argument. I thought you two being friends would chill you both out, but if you renegotiate the breakdown of the presentation, I'm gone." We all laugh. It's true to mine and Lisa's relationship. We do argue a lot.

"Fine, but we aren't planning to celebrate early either" I conclude glaring at Kate.

Kate throws her hands up exasperated. "Fine, we won't plan to 'celebrate,' but what are you guys doing next weekend?"

"We have plans." Ben says, lacing his fingers through mine and giving them a squeeze. I turn to him smiling.

"What plans do we have?" I giggle a little.

"Plans that don't involve the three musketeers. I already have to miss hanging out with you this weekend, and I have to share you with them in class. I get you to myself next weekend. Besides, it's our 3-month anniversary."

"It is?" Kate and I say in unison. Then Kate finishes her sentence. "How disgusting."

"Yeah, I mean, it's 3 months from the fall festival." He shrugs. I feel silly for not knowing that. How did I miss we have been dating for three months? I look up into Ben's eyes. The way he looks at me is like he's telling me a secret. Like I get a part of him that no one else does.

"Well, how are we celebrating?" I ask.

"Hold on, hold on, hold on," Kate rants. "I thought planning to celebrate in advance jinxes things?"

I sigh. "You are exhausting."

She smiles. "No, I'm right."

The ringing of the bell prevents me from having to debate with her. Kate's a lot, in a good way. I keep wanting to get her and Sarah Mae together, but with my school schedule and Sarah Mae going to the gallery almost every weekend now, it's hard to meet up. While I make new friends at Briarwood, my old life slips away.

Ben breaks me from my thoughts by pulling me into one of the study alcoves to the side.

"I'm going to meet my mom and Brody at the treatment center. Are you good on your own for lunch?" he asks, and I'm confused. Ben's mom normally only has treatment on Mondays.

"Yeah, but is everything okay?" I search his face for any tell that something is amiss. He doesn't look upset.

"No, no, it's good news. Mom got into a trial for a new drug, and we are meeting with her doctor for her first dose."

"Wait. Ben that's amazing! Why didn't you tell me?"

"I just found out before class. I didn't want to bring it up in front of Kate and Lisa." Realization hits me. Not everyone knows about Ben's mom. He has been private about it.

"I understand." I lean up and give him a quick kiss. "Go ahead, I'll go grab something from the cafeteria. Will you be back for Anatomy?"

"Probably not, but I'll come back by before the end of the day. I want to say a proper goodbye before you leave for the weekend." I know what Ben means by a proper goodbye. He has never pushed the physical aspect of our relationship, but that doesn't stop us from making out in my car.

I smile up at him. "Can't wait. Good sir." I curtsy.

"My lady" he bows then turns heel and walks off.

Three months. I've been dating Ben for three months. It feels short and longer at the same time. When I think back to how I made myself all those rules starting out here I laugh. I didn't really need them. My grades are up. I have friends. I have a boyfriend. Maybe just maybe I can have the whole high school experience.

# Chapter 30

I spoke in front of two thousand people and didn't vomit! Today will go down in the history books! Okay maybe not, but Lisa and I killed our presentation. Also, Mr. Bannerman is a lying liar. He told us we were speaking in front of a couple hundred people. It was two thousand. We addressed the entire conference. I was shaking by the time we got off the stage. Then there waiting as we exit the stage is Mr. Bannerman smiling a big smile that says he got away with something.

Here's the thing. I'm an amazing writer. I know it. I am fine with knowing it because I'm not the best public speaker. I can hide behind pen and paper or my keyboard any day. However, addressing hundreds of people much less thousands, is, needless to say, outside of my comfort zone. Thankfully, Lisa took the first part of the presentation. I never thought four months ago I would want to kiss her face out of gratitude. An expression of course. I'm pretty sure that the quiet Bella would punch me if I actually kissed her. She may be timid, but I have a feeling she could put me in my place if she were angry enough.

Now that the fear of presenting is far behind me, I'm ready to celebrate. What better way to celebrate than go to every single booth in the conference and collect freebies? NYU has a booth somewhere around here. They have a partnership with the New York Times. I can't wait to make it to their representative and as it turns out I don't have to. As I make my way out of the crowd, I'm stopped my Mr. Bannerman and the previously mentioned rep.

"Miss Roberts, I have someone who is eager to meet you" Mr. Bannerman says.

I instinctively reach my hand out and shake the hand of a woman in a navy skirt suit with a gold NYU tag visible on her blazer. "Hello, I'm Amelia Roberts."

"I'm aware Miss Roberts; it's a pleasure to finally meet you in person. I'm Olivia Jones. I've read several of your articles. It's good to put a face to the voice," she speaks with authority, and I'm about to faint.

"Thank you, ma'am" I respond politely. Olivia Jones, head recruiter for NYU has read my articles.

"Well, if you have some time I would like to sit down for a cup of coffee and discuss a future for you at NYU. Mr. Bannerman tells me that we are at the top of your list." I smile gratefully at Mr. Bannerman. This makes up for him lying about how many people we would speak in front of.

"I would love that."

"Well, I'll leave you ladies to it. I need to go track down Miss Taylor. There is a Harvard rep that I want her to meet." With that he leaves us.

"Like Harvard needs any help," Ms. Jones rolls her eyes.

"Not a fan of the Ivy," I joke. It just came out. What? I'm nervous.

"It seems you aren't either" she responds. I breathe a sigh of relief that she took it well.

"No ma'am, I have always wanted to go to NYU." I clarify.

"Ma'am, I'm not much older than you. You can call me Olivia."

"Yes ma'am." I stop myself. "Sorry, force of habit. It's the south after all."

"That it is." She motions me to follow her and leads us out of the large conference room to a small coffee kiosk that has been set up outside. After we both get our cups and exchange some basic pleasantries, we sit down to begin. I'm not sure what is worse, the nerves from giving the presentation or this conversation.

"I have to ask. With your grades and early success in the field, what interests you in NYU versus the Ivy League?" Wow, she is straight to the point.

"Honestly. New York. I've loved the city since I was a little girl. My mom would take me once a year. When I was old enough to read, I'd beg her to get me a copy of The New

York Times from the news stand." I remember the feel of the first paper I bought. I can smell the ink. "New York is where my love of journalism was born, and your school is one of the few that works with the Times. Your journalism program is unmatched." I hope my answer is what she is looking for.

"You are an interesting young lady. Most students would have highlighted only how NYU would be lucky to have them or how it is a steppingstone for great things." I take a moment to ponder what she has said. I've never looked at NYU as a steppingstone. It's a destination. Have I been short-sighted?

"NYU has been my goal for years. I want to experience everything it has to offer. I'd be grateful to attend your school. I just hope you can see some value in me and my writing and allot me the opportunity." My response is earnest. It's never been a given that I'll be accepted.

"Unmatched talent, yet humble. Keep that attitude when you join our ranks." she says impressed.

"Join your ranks?" My heart is beating fast. I don't think I heard her correctly.

"Oh, I intend to offer you early admissions. Amelia, you are one of the most talented writers I've seen in years. I came to this conference for you. I've been corresponding with Mr. Bannerman the last couple of months." As she speaks my mouth hangs open.

"I'm not sure what to say. Thank you."

"It is conditional of course. You have to keep your grades up and remain on the Briarwood paper. I'll be checking in every couple of months just to make sure you stay on track."

"Yes ma'am, I mean Olivia," she laughs as I fumble.

Just like that, every dream I have been working for comes true. I'm going to the college of my dreams. I knew Briarwood would help me get there but I never thought it would happen this fast. I can't wait to tell my mom. I have to thank Mr. Bannerman. Ben. I want to tell Ben.

# Chapter 31

After finishing the conference, thanking Mr. Bannerman repeatedly to the point he sent me away, Lisa and I settled into our room. She had a good conversation with the Harvard rep too. She's been locked in the bathroom on the phone with Bella for the last hour giving me ample time to video call my mom. There was screaming, dancing, and a promise to celebrate as soon as I get home. No answer from Ben. I check my messages and there isn't a text either. I'm starting to worry by the time curfew hits. He's supposed to pick me up in the morning.

Laying down to sleep I shoot a text to Alyssa to see if Brody has heard from him. As soon as the message hits delivered my phone rings and Alyssa's contact picture flashes on the screen. I answer immediately.

"Hey Alyssa. What's up?" I ask.

"Amelia, where are you?" Her voice is serious. My stomach plummets.

"I'm in my hotel room. Why?"

"Are you alone?" she asks. Something is wrong. It has to be.

"No, Lisa is with me. Why?" At the mention of her name Lisa sits up in bed and mouths 'Are you okay?' to me. I shrug.

"Okay. I'm going to tell you something and you can't freak out or try to rush home." Alyssa continues.

"Alyssa, you're scaring me. What's wrong? Is it Grace? Is Ben okay?" This is bad, I can feel it.

"No Grace is fine." she answers. Relief washes over me. "Ben was in an accident." The panic takes over.

"What do you mean he was in accident? Where? Where is he? If he is okay? Why didn't he answer the phone?" Lisa gets out of bed and comes over to me.

"I promise he's going to be okay." She tries to comfort me. Going to be is not the same as is. "He was on his bike coming home from the treatment center. A kid ran a red light and hit him." The world starts to spin. "He broke his arm and had to have surgery on his wrist, which is where he is now. Nothing is life-threatening."

"What hospital?" My body starts moving faster than my mind can process. I'm up and pulling my suitcase out.

"Amelia, you can't come in the middle of the night. It will be safer for you to wait until the morning. Ben asked us not to tell you until after your presentation." Her words stop me in my tracks. My boyfriend gets hit by a car, breaks his arm, has to have surgery and was worried about my presentation! I'm going to kill him, then kiss him, then more murder.

"Alyssa, what hospital? I can go wake Mr. Bannerman up or I can get on a bus. I'll Uber there if I have to." I exclaim.

"He's at Briarwood Memorial. Don't try and Uber. It's a four-hour drive. Give me some time and I'll work something out." she says.

"Fine but if you don't call me back in 30 minutes, I'm getting an Uber." What I would give to be able to click my heels three times right now.

I didn't get an Uber. Alyssa called my mom. It took her and Lisa trying to calm me down before Lisa gave up and went and got Mr. Bannerman. She very persuasively got him to agree to drive us back. The whole car ride is a blur. I vaguely remember Lisa patting my hand telling me it was going to be okay. She isn't very good at comfort, but I appreciate her snapping into action and getting me back to Briarwood.

Mom meets us in the parking lot of the hospital. I collapse in her arms but quickly collect myself to go inside. I'm met in a waiting room by Brody and Alyssa. Ben's dad having just left to go update his mom in person. Grace is probably out of her mind. She can't risk catching anything by coming to the hospital.

When I arrive, it's all hugs and they both assured me the surgery went well. They say I can go back and see him, but

I'm nervous. Mom asks if I want her to go with me. I opt to leave her in the lobby.

I regret the decision when I see him in the bed. He has a cut over his left eye, and I notice bruises all over. His arm is wrapped in gauze and his curls are tossed even crazier than normal. Tears start streaming as I approach his bed. He looks frail. Weak. His usual smile lays hidden behind a flat line on his mouth. Ben's eyes open slowly, then a half smile peaks out. He tries to move and winces.

"Hey Dorothy. Guess what? I fought a tornado. It won." I laugh. Ben is high. God, I love him. Pause. I do. I love Ben.

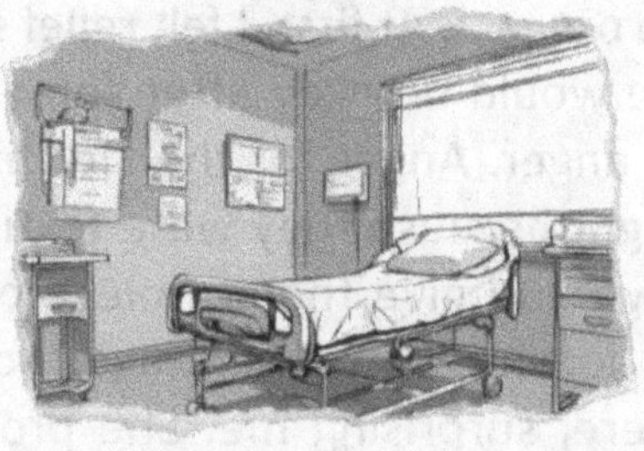

# Chapter 32

I spent the night in a chair beside Ben's hospital bed. Brody and Alyssa didn't argue. Mom, knowing me too well, just said she would bring me a change of clothes in the morning and to text if I needed anything. Eventually, Alyssa went home, and Brody had a second chair brought in for him. Their dad gave the doctors permission for Brody to act as guardian in his absence. I knew Brody and Ben were close, but the way he watches over Ben now it seems he has become less of a brother and more of a father figure to Ben.

I haven't slept much. Nurses keep coming in and out to check vitals. At about 4 am I give up on sleep. As quietly as I can, I leave my chair and exit the room to use the restroom in the waiting area. While Ben's room has a private restroom, I don't want to risk waking him or Brody. Ben's night was rough. Even though he slept a lot, he stays groggy from the meds. He would wake up in pain often. In addition to breaking his wrist, he also bruised several ribs, and sustained a concussion. He kept complaining of a headache until they took him for a CT. Thank God everything looked normal.

It's been a lot to process. At first, I felt relief seeing him alive and knowing he would be okay after some recovery time. Then came the anger. Anger for the kid that was careless and ran a red light because they were texting. I wanted to track them down and give them a piece of my mind if it wouldn't mean leaving Ben. Lisa stayed for a little while after we got here, surprising me. She promised me that justice would be served and now I feel bad for the kid. I'm also angry at Ben a little, for not letting anyone tell me sooner. Then there is the other feeling, the unfamiliar one.

My entire life, I've been afraid of love. My mom loved my dad. We see how that turned out. He's off in his perfect world with a new family pretending I never existed. Sure, there's a birthday card here and there but what is that compared to a relationship? I love my mom and I love our life. Still, the thought of ever putting myself or much less a kid through what we went through is scary. Yeah, I'm only 16 and I'm sure everyone has a first love, but this is still terrifying. The thought of losing Ben or something happening to him shattered me. I can't imagine a life without him. Something clicked the day I met Ben; it was like my world shifted into place. I fought it out of the pretense of needing to focus on school but in reality, I fought it out of fear or repeating my mom's past.

Which is crazy. Ben wouldn't do what my dad did. At least, I don't think he would.

As I slip back into Ben's room, he is sitting up in the bed. His eyes are more alert than they have been all night.

"Hey there Dorothy. Early riser?" His voice is hoarse, and I move to get him some water from his bedside tray.

"Sorry. Did I wake you?" I lift the water to his lips, and he takes a long swig.

"Thank you. No, Brody's snoring woke me." He nods to the side as he whispers and Brody snoozes softly. Not too loud, but enough it could have woken him.

"How are you feeling? Sorry, that's a stupid question. Of course, you can't be feeling too great." Ben grabs my hand that is hanging by my side to stop me.

"Slow down. I'm fine. Little banged up, but that's all better now that my guardian angel is here."

"Ha, some guardian angel I am. I probably look like a bridge troll after sleeping in that chair."

"Yes, but you're a very pretty troll." Ben laughs then winces.

"Serves you right." I snicker. "Seriously though, how are you?"

"It hurts, but the pain killers they're giving me help. It isn't until they wear off that I have a problem." As he talks, I brush some of the hair out of his eyes remembering how I wanted to twirl one of his curls around my finger the first day I met him. So, I do. "That's helping." he leans into my touch.

"Eventually, not now, but eventually we are going to have to talk about how you told people not to tell me that you were in an accident." My voice a little stern but not much.

"I didn't want to ruin your presentation. You've worked for months on it."

"That is beside the point. If something happens to you, I want to know immediately. Regardless, we can talk about it when you're feeling better. That way I can hit you." I continue twirling his curls around my finger and attempt to keep my voice at a whisper.

"My answer won't change later. I stand by it because I bet the presentation went well, didn't it?"

"Not the point."

"Didn't it?"

"Yeah, it did." I smile a little. "But we are focused on you right now."

"No," Ben carefully lifts his non-injured arm and grabs my wrist, pulling me to sit on the side of the bed. I try to sit as carefully as I can, not bumping him. "I want to focus on you, people have been focused on me too much."

"Oh no, it's like you almost died." I quip. He's annoyingly stubborn.

"That's dramatic. I didn't almost die. I just got hit by a car." We both laugh, he winces again, and Brody stirs. We stop and stare at him until he settles again. "Really Amelia, tell me something to distract me."

"Fine. It went really well. There weren't hundreds of people, there were thousands, and after I got to have coffee with the NYU rep." I continue playing with his hair.

"That's great! What did she say?" He tries to sit up more but stops himself. I frown, but he continues. "I'm fine. What did she say?"

The joy from the conversation with the rep returns and a small smile forms on my lips "She offered me early admissions."

"Dorothy, are you serious? I knew it, I knew you could do it. Early admissions as a junior, that's unheard of. I'm so proud of you." He tries to sit up and kiss me but leans back in pain.

"Would you stop that?" I scold.

"Will you come here so I can get a kiss?" he pouts. "I almost died. I should at least get a kiss."

"Oh, now he almost dies?" I tease and Ben tugs on my hand. I lean over and carefully plant a kiss on his lips and my whole heart explodes. I want to tell him; I want to tell him I love him, but I can't. I don't want him to think it is only because of where he's at right now. As I sit up, I look at him in the eyes and there it is. My special look.

"Dorothy, I want to tell you something." Ben takes a slow breath and steadies himself. "I've wanted to tell you for a while but I didn't want to scare you and I don't want you to

206

think I'm saying it just because I was hit by a car and I don't want you to leave me now that I'm all broken." Oh my god. He is not. My breath catches. Can he read my mind? "You are the most amazing girl I've ever met. You are witty and funny. You don't take my shit and man am I nervous." His ranting is adorable, and I almost want to put him out of his misery. "Oh hell, I love you."

I don't wait, I don't pause. "I love you too." His face lights up. "I wanted to tell you too, but I didn't want you to think I was saying it just because you are in a hospital bed."

"You love me too?"

"I do."

It's true. I do love Ben. It's a real all-consuming kind of love. He balances me. He supports me. He respects me. It helps that he's hot. I love everything about Ben. At 16 I met the love of my life. At least that is the way it feels right now. I love Ben. Ben loves me. It's simple really. I don't know if this is something that will last a lifetime or if this is a first love burning bright. Whatever it is, I'm going to enjoy it. I'm going to enjoy living this life. New set of rules, don't try to set rules because life is going to happen, and it doesn't care about your rules. Just take what comes.

One week from Ben's accident marks our 3-month anniversary. He doesn't seem to understand that getting hit by a car precedes any plans he made. After two days in the hospital, he was released and told to take it easy. Something I'm learning is not in his vocabulary. A gap in the Briarwood curriculum. He insists that we will still go on our date, playing up the "almost died" card anytime I try to argue. I don't know what he has planned, but he's determined not to give it up.

He even talked Brody into playing chauffeur in his new, very safe truck that he bought him. While it is too soon for him to drive with his wrist injury, I think the purchase has to do with Alyssa and Brody insisting that he never drive a motorcycle again. I second that decision.

We are now in the back of the previously mentioned truck, with me sitting opposite his injured wrist so we can hold hands. I'm in my favorite green flowy dress and comfy black sweater. Ben's wearing dark jeans and a black sweater. He looks desperately handsome, and the cut over his eye makes him look like the cover of a dark romance novel. He could have just competed in an underground boxing tournament or fought off a rival gang. I use that comparison anytime he worries over the cut.

Despite refusing to take any more painkillers, he's been a ball of energy the entire night. Of course, I have been given no details. Mom knows and won't tell. Alyssa was useless too. I think even Kate and Sarah Mae know something. They finally met, by the way. At the hospital, and just as I expected, they get along well. I can't seem to find time to hang out with Sarah Mae, but she and Kate already made plans to go to the gallery together. Kate surprised me with a hidden talent for sketching. I was shocked when she showed Sarah Mae some of her stuff. They are more similar than I thought. I'm working hard not to be offended, knowing that Ben does take up a lot of my time.

The truck turns into the same open field as the fall festival, and that is when I see the lights. The Winter Carnival isn't supposed to start for a few days, but here in the middle of the event grounds, all the rides are set up. It's beautiful. The Ferris wheel stands tall above everything else.

"Ben," I squeeze his hand.

"I couldn't think of a better way to celebrate our 3-month anniversary than in Kansas," Ben leans over and kisses the top of my forehead. I'm shocked. Never in a million years would I have expected this. I don't even want to think of the logistics behind putting this together. I'm bouncing up and down in my seat with excitement. It's then I see the other cars. I recognize all of them. Sarah Mae's, Kate's, my mom's. What in the world?

I don't wait for Ben to be a gentleman and open my door, something he grumbles at me about and Brody laughs, asking him what he expected. Sure enough, at the entrance, stands all my friends, my mom, Alyssa, and even Grace is here. I turn shocked to Ben.

"I figured that we could enjoy this night all to ourselves, or we could enjoy it with all of our friends and family." I thought I realized Ben was perfect when we had our first back-and-forth, but no, it is the moment that he included all the people we love in our special night. If we were older, I would think he was going to propose. That would be crazy.

Hand in hand, we walk into the carnival grounds. There isn't a full staff, but there are enough people working so that all the rides are active. Ben's injury limits him from going on everything, but it doesn't stop him from cheering as I smash into Lisa on the bumper cars. Hey, just because we are friends doesn't mean there aren't some hard feelings to work out still.

The whole night we laugh and talk. I notice my mom and Grace eating cotton candy and laughing together. Grace looks good. I was worried about her being out in the cold, but it doesn't seem to be bothering her.

Kate, Sarah Mae, Lisa, and Bella huddle up, and it is bizarre seeing my two worlds collide. Sarah Mae did threaten Lisa with her life if she ever spoke sideways to me again. It was entertaining because Lisa backed down. Lisa continues to surprise me. It helps that she and Bella can openly hold hands and be together here. No one will say anything. Aside from a strange glance from Ben and me shaking my head to him not to say anything, no one has acknowledged it.

As I approach the group, I hear Kate "Tell her now. It's the perfect time."

"Tell her what?" I ask.

"Sarah Mae has something she wants to tell you." Kate answers pushing Sarah Mae toward me.

"Not now." Sarah Mae tells her. "Tonight isn't about me."

"Okay, now you have to tell me." I say.

Sarah May glares at Kate then turns back to me "Ugh. Fine. I want to preface this with I'm not trying to take away from your anniversary."

"Okay, no need. Now tell me." I reply.

"So, I didn't tell you because I wasn't sure it would happen, but I applied to Briarwood."

"You what?!" I exclaim.

"And I got in under the recruitment program." She says nonchalantly.

I squeal and throw my arms around her. "I'm so proud of you! This is amazing. When do you start?"

She hugs me back. "First of the semester".

"Oh great." Ben says "More people to share her with."

"Hush Ben." Kate chastises "You know you love us."

"Sure." he says. "Okay. We are very happy for you, but I have one more surprise for Amelia."

I give him my own award-winning smile then turn back to Sarah Mae ecstatic "We can talk more tomorrow? Breakfast at my place?"

"Absolutely. I'll place my order with Gabriel now." she laughs.

After I few more words, Ben pulls me to the Ferris wheel. It's the one ride he can go on without getting jostled around.

I wrap my hand in his, sitting and look around at the scene. Our friends having fun, Ben looking relaxed, happy, and very proud of himself.

"This is amazing Ben. Thank you" I peck his cheek.

"It isn't over yet" he smiles a big, silly smile.

"Benedict Blake, what else could you have planned that would top all of this? I still want to know how you pulled this off" I gesture around the carnival grounds as the Ferris wheel shuffles us around.

"A gentleman never tells." He offers.

"Really?" I raise my brow.

"Okay, Okay. Your mom helped. She was planning the event anyway. She called in a favor. Originally, I was only supposed to bring you a few hours before they opened, but she talked them into letting us have it the night before. Your mom is persuasive."

"That she is." I smile.

"Besides Dorothy, you can't keep comparing me to the lead in all those romance novels you read without me living up to it." As he speaks, he pulls a small box from his pocket and my breath catches. He is not. Horror streaks my face.

"Calm down, Dorothy. I'm not proposing," he opens the box to display a beautiful pendant on a necklace. The necklace holds six stones that start large at the bottom and get smaller to the top. "It's called a journey necklace. It's meant to mark special occasions as you move throughout life" he explains, handing me the box.

"Ben, I love it." I really do. It's perfect. I move to take it out of the box. I attempt to hold it to put it on. Ben moves to hold my hair out of the way with his uninjured hand. "Thank you. It's perfect."

"You're perfect," he scrubs his hair. "I heard how cheesy it sounded, but it's true."

"You are pretty perfect too." We are a scene out of a movie, and I love it. I lean in and kiss him.

"Really Amelia, this year was going to suck. Between my mom being sick and me screwing up, I thought I'd get stuck mentoring some freshman kid. Then I get you as a mentee, and that was just about the luckiest day of my life."

"I'm the lucky one. I know we haven't talked about it much, but between my dad and the disaster that was Tyler, my confidence in dating had been wrecked. Then I get assigned this really cute and funny mentor that brings me coffee."

"See I knew it was the coffee."

"Ha Ha. Seriously. I'm really happy because of you."

"I'm really happy too, Dorothy."

"I love you." The Ferris wheel stops.

"I love you too."

And in my own personal romcom, the scene fades with me kissing my boyfriend at the top of the Ferris wheel. I couldn't have written a better ending myself.

Obviously, the story can't end. I'm 16, technically I'm 17 now. A birthday that was celebrated in true Roberts' women fashion. With a trip to New York. I got to go meet with Ms. Jones and tour the campus. Even better news, because Sarah Mae and I haven't spent as much time together with her classes not matching mine, she came with us. Blown away by their art program, she is thinking of applying. I know she had her heart set on Savannah College of Art and Design, but it would be incredible to have her here with me in the city. I would feel less alone.

As for me and Ben, we are still going strong. I thought when I left Wilcocks that I would miss out on the normal high school experiences. I never imagined that I would have that at Briarwood. But here I am in the back of a limo going to prom. The collection of people fills me with joy. I have Kate, Lisa, Bella, Sarah Mae (Kate and Sarah Mae have their dates too, but I'm not counting them, they picked them up in art class), and Ben. Bella came out to her mom. It went better than anyone could have expected. She was more open to things after the divorce. Lisa's parents are still a problem, but mom has offered to let her stay with us anytime she needs a break.

We haven't even arrived at the venue and the night has already been incredible. Gabriel cooked us a remarkable meal at the inn before we ventured out. Mom set up a photographer for a glamour shoot for all the girls. I wasn't into the idea at first, but it ended up being a good time.

Ben is in a classic tux that continues the image of him as Mr. Romcom, a nickname I proudly call him to his face now. He doesn't mind.

The last few months have been tough for him. He healed fine after his accident, but his mom's new treatment has had mixed results. It got worse before it got better. There were a lot of weekends spent at the treatment facility, and she had to move in there for some of it. Ben didn't want to leave her side at times, not sure if it would be her last moments. I admire his dedication to her, but it's aged him. Over the last month, she has made a turn for the better. She was able to come home and can get around some without her wheelchair. It's truly incredible. Her last scans looked good too.

With senior year and talk of college looming over us, I'm worried about what will happen to our relationship. I can't see Ben wanting to go away to college with his mom's health in question. I'm going to NYU; that has never been a question, and Ben has done nothing but been supportive. I just hope that this next year doesn't put a strain on our relationship. Things have been going really well.

Even with all the thoughts and uncertainty about the future, I've decided to enjoy whatever time we do have together before it could all end, and tonight is included in that.

"Ready to go cut up the dance floor, Dorothy?" Ben says as he takes my hand to help me out of the limo.

"Ready," I smile up at him.

I am ready. Ready for tonight and whatever our future brings. After all, this is our story, and I intend to live it.

**Benedict**

I thought I might die there for a second. I would never tell Amelia or anyone else how afraid I was when that car hit me. The blinding pain or the thinking the headlights were different lights. Then like an angel, Amelia appeared by my bedside. I can't believe how lucky I am to have her. She has stayed with me through everything this year. Spending time with me in the treatment facility with my mom. Watching me break down and holding me when we thought we would lose her.

She's inspiring in how she treats other people and how clever she is. I knew she was bound for greatness. NYU is just the start for her. I want to be there to watch her get everything in life she wants. I'll be there in the front row cheering her on, but I can't ignore the fact that mom won't last long. The last few weeks she seems like she feels better, but that has happened before.

So I'm stuck. At least we have one more year together before we have to face that issue. I haven't told her I applied to Princeton. I don't want to get her hopes up. Even being a legacy and with my grades up it's a long shot. I will take tonight. I'll enjoy dancing with my stunning girlfriend. She calls me her Mr. Romcom but what she doesn't know is that not a single girl in any romcom can hold a candle to her. She is my Dorothy, and I can't wait to go on any adventure she wants, even if we get caught in a few tornadoes on the way.

# Acknowledgements

Thank you reader for taking the time to read my story. I have wanted to be a writer since I was a little girl. That dream drifted farther away as I got older and older. Now a little past 30 I am so pleased to make this dream come true with you.

I also want to thank my Valkyrie sisters. I never could have written this book without you. You all have been my rocks through this whole process. I love you. Thank you for letting me be me and showing me that it's beautiful.

Jesse, thank you for loving me and supporting me. Thank you for staying up with me the late nights of editing, and for inspiring Ben. You are my original Mr. Romcom.

Mom, thank you for being an inspiration. Thank you for being the role model that I needed and for always pushing me to achieve my full potential.

To all the girls who read this book. Love can come your way at any moment. It is important to find the balance between love and your dreams. Find someone to share your life with that holds the same values as you, that wants more for you, and that will support you. Don't ever settle for less. Know your value. You deserve it all.

# About the Author

Logan Schober was raised in Darlington, Florida. She grew up with her mom and three older brothers. From an early age she wanted to be a writer. She attended Florida State University.

After college she relocated to Georgia with her Husband, Jesse Schober. They have two beautiful children together.

Currently, Logan channels her creative energy and love for language as a dedicated middle grades English teacher. Through her role, she not only imparts knowledge but also ignites the flame of curiosity and appreciation for literature in the hearts of her students.

Despite the demands of her profession and the responsibilities of motherhood, Logan has never let go of her dream of becoming a published author. Her debut work stands as a testament to her perseverance and unwavering dedication to storytelling.

With immense joy and gratitude, Logan Schober welcomes readers into the world she has crafted, inviting them to embark on a journey of imagination and emotion. Through her words, she hopes to inspire, uplift, and touch the hearts of all who delve into her stories.

www.ingramcontent.com/pod-product-compliance
Lightning Source LLC
Chambersburg PA
CBHW011142310726
48972CB00009B/2820